P9-CQV-250

D - 2000
9 -

# CHILDREN OF THE WOLF

ALSO BY JANE YOLEN

*The Gift of Sarah Barker*

*Simple Gifts: The Story of the Shakers*

# CHILDREN
# OF THE WOLF

◆◆◆

## A NOVEL BY
## JANE YOLEN

THE VIKING PRESS, NEW YORK

For my son Jason Stemple, who loves
all of nature

And for Linda Zuckerman
and Deborah Brodie,
who ask the right questions

Copyright © 1984 by Jane Yolen
All rights reserved · First published in 1984 by The Viking Press
40 West 23rd Street, New York, New York 10010
Published simultaneously in Canada by Penguin Books Canada Limited
Printed in U.S.A.    4   5   88   87   86

Library of Congress Cataloging in Publication Data
Yolen, Jane.      Children of the wolf.
Summary: In 1920 in India two children who have been raised
by wolves are discovered and brought to an orphanage to be taught
human behavior again.
[1. Feral children—Fiction.   2. India—Fiction] I. Title.
PZ7.Y78Ch   1984   [Fic]   83-16979   ISBN 0-670-21763-8

# CONTENTS

◆◆◆

# CHILDREN OF THE WOLF

# RAMA AND ME

###### ◆◆◆

A WOLF BARKED OUTSIDE UNDER THE WINDOW OF THE
bedroom that Rama and I shared. It woke me out of an
uneasy sleep. I had been dozing when what I really
wanted to do was wait up for Rama's return.

I opened my eyes, and the first thing I saw was the
moon shining in the window, making a mark on Rama's
empty bed. It was a stark, accusing finger, that white
light, but if Rama had been there at that moment to see
it, he would have shrugged it away. He did not care if
anyone knew he sneaked out of The Home at night to
go out dancing and drinking in the village. He wore his

3

new manhood easily, as proud of it as a soldier of his colored riband medals.

The wolf barked again, and I sat up. I shivered, though it was hot, the beginning of the rainless season. Rather than stare at the window where the wolf waited, I stared at Rama's bed. If only I dared to go out with him, to sing and dance to the music of the wailing *narh* and the pounding beat of the tabor drum; to parade with him on the back streets of Tantigoria and sit in the little bazaar drinking green coconut water or homemade wine.

I shivered once more, not knowing if I was more afraid of the wolf outside or of the village men, wondering if they were all made more dreadful because of imagination. Even at fourteen I was more boy than man, more dreamer than doer, making monsters where there were none.

The wolf barked a third time, and then the bark turned into a giggle.

"Rama!" I whispered fiercely.

"Mo-han-das," came a ghostly voice from the compound.

Of course, no wolf could have gotten in, past the great wooden gates and fence, past the dogs which roamed loose at night inside the compound. Even though we lived close by the great sal jungle, we had no fear of wild animals. Between us and the sal lay first the *maidan*, the parade grounds, and then the rice fields. They served as further defenses. Civilization, we Indians knew, was an effective barrier to beasts.

All the fears I had conjured up disappeared. I would have laughed at myself if Rama had not already laughed at me. Wolf, indeed!

Rama climbed in the window and sat on the sill, his long, strong legs dangling down almost to the floor.

"You were not afraid of a wolf, Mohandas?" he teased.

"They steal children," I said. "I am not a child."

He nodded. We knew all about wolves. There was not a village in the sal jungle that did not have a story about a child taken from its mother's side as she gathered firewood or picked herbs. But I had no mother to be stolen from. And I was *not* a child.

"And you are no wolf," I added aloud.

"I am the wolf of Tantigoria," he said in English, smiling that sweet, wide smile that had all of us at The Home ready to do his bidding. Then he switched to Bengali, the tongue of his own people, and described what had happened that night.

I lay back and listened, closing my eyes so that he might think I had fallen asleep, but I heard it all. In Bengali, which he spoke with grace and ease, the tale was full of village rhythms. He even sang a song about the end of the rains.

I knew I would write it down in my notebook in the cipher hand I had devised, come morning.

Once Rama had read out to the others what I had written in my book. The Reverend Mr. Welles had given each of us a book in which to practice our English writing. I made up stories and bits and pieces of poems, and sometimes I wrote down things about the other children. About Rama, who had been nearly eight when his dying grandmother had brought him to The Home, who spoke Bengali like a singer and English like a fool. About Krithi, who had a shriveled leg and so had been left in the forest by his parents when he was an infant and found by an Englishman on *shikar*. About Veda, who had been picked up unclaimed from the streets of Santalia and who braided the *pipal* flowers in her hair but did not speak above a whisper. About Preeti, whose seeing was shadowed and who had to look from the corners of her eyes. About the dark anger of Indira, no orphan at all, whose parents had sent her to The Home to be schooled and who loved to pinch the younger girls until they cried out loud.

Rama had performed nearly half a page of my poetry in his halting English in front of the others, his voice still cracking from his manhood change, before I had had the courage to leap on him, hitting and kicking, screaming curses in Bengali, though the language is forbidden in The Home. Rama laughed and apologized and returned the book to me. Not because I had hurt him. None of the rest of us was strong enough for that. But because he was not mean by nature. He returned the book, I think, because he had judged how much anger there was in me. He did not know that it was not anger but fear, fear that he would read out what I had written about him—about his beauty and his power over all of us children—and that armed with that knowledge he would somehow be changed.

That was when I invented my cipher hand, a code part English, part Bengali, and part made-up words with which to hide my innermost thoughts. But it did not matter that I wrote it in cipher. Rama never again tried to look at my book, nor would he let any of the others. The one time Indira tried, he shook her like a puppy until she dropped it. The other girls cheered—even Veda—and Indira's face turned nearly black with loathing. But her anger was toward me, not Rama. None of us could be angry with him.

The mornings after one of Rama's night wanderings always came too early. We were expected to perform many chores at The Home: weeding the kitchen garden, emptying the trash, cleaning up after the dogs. Rama and I, being the oldest boys, had the most arduous tasks, but even the little ones had their duties.

Rama got up easily, as supple as a jungle cat, stretching and moving comfortably. I always had to be shaken awake.

"Come, Mohandas, quickly, or there will be another speech." Rama hated the English words that poured so easily from Mr. Welles' mouth. "A waterfall of words," Rama often said with disgust. "Someday we will all drown in them." It was unusual for Rama to display such imagination. He mistrusted words, especially the English ones. His was a language of touch and laughter. Was it any wonder that the one person not under Rama's spell was Mr. Welles?

I nodded reluctantly. To me the words that flowed so easily out of Mr. Welles were a miracle. They matched the words I could read in books. I only hoped that someday there would be some way to unlock the flood of words that was stopped up inside of me. I wanted to pour those words out. But I did not let Rama—or anyone else—know of this.

I got up and dressed quickly, and with the *kharom* on our feet clickety-clacking on the floor as we walked, we went out of our room.

As always, I was aware of what a strange pair we made—brothers and not brothers. By chance kin and friends. By chance only, the dark and unhappy forces that had brought us to this place had bound us to each other for seven years, like someone in the Bible. He was so tall and smiling, his handsome face mobile and open. And I was his small, brown, smileless shadow, always a step behind.

We reported, as usual, with all the other children to the hall near the kitchen, where Mr. Welles waited. Showered and brushed and polished, even in a jungle setting, the Reverend Mr. Welles gleamed.

"We are here, sir," I said, speaking in English for Rama as well as myself.

Rama smiled.

The other children bowed.

And so, as always, began our day.

Mr. Welles put out his white hands, too white, for the sun never seemed to change them, the palms turned up as if receiving a gift from the skies. We did the same. In a great circle before him, we children stood for five long, silent minutes and prayed. For me the silence was no chore, though for some of the younger ones it was an agony. Often I watched them under lowered lids as they tried not to shift from one foot to another. Krithi, with one leg noticeably shorter than the other, always had the worst time. But Mr. Welles was strict on that account, even with Krithi.

After the silence Mr. Welles preached at us for another five minutes, most of the time about duty, though occasionally about other things. And then at last we were set free to attend to our chores. That was how it was every day.

But the day I remember best was the one that began with the barking man-wolf and the moon's outstretched finger. I remember it because it was different from the rest, the day that began the strange events that unraveled all our lives, for it was the day that the man from Godamuri appeared.

# GHOSTS

◆◆◆

THE VILLAGE OF GODAMURI LIES UNCOMFORTABLY BETWEEN the city of Midnapore and the Morbhanj border on the edge of the great sal jungle. It is a small, insignificant place of very primitive people, or so Mr. Welles said. He had visited it many times on his missionary tours. But insignificant or not, Godamuri was a thorn in his side, for he had not been able to convert a single villager to the god Christ. They were Hindus there, and ghost worshipers.

The village was so poor that, even though each house had a courtyard and a cowshed, Mr. Welles preferred to stay overnight in the sheds rather than in the houses.

"It is infinitely more comfortable," he said, adding as a quiet afterthought, "and cleaner, too. And better company." The last was said only to his lady wife. I overheard it, although I think I was not supposed to. Better company the cows probably were. They, at least, did not believe in ghosts.

It was because of a particular ghost, a *manush-bagha*, a man-ghost, that we made the trip that fall day in 1920 to Godamuri—Mr. Welles, Rama, several carters, and I. The villagers had become so frightened of this *manush-bagha* that they sent one of their number to The Home. They hoped that Mr. Welles, being a Christian and a good hunter, might come and frighten the *manush-bagha* away.

The man who came from Godamuri was named Chunarem. He was a small and wiry dark man, with a face marked clearly by a succession of diseases. ("A veritable map of smallpox," Mrs. Welles later said. I wrote that down in my book.) He made a steeple of his fingers, lowered his head to greet Mr. Welles, and spoke like this:

"It is hideous, *sahib*, and only partly human. Its body and hands and feet are like a little man's. Its head is enormous." He rubbed his own head vigorously as he spoke.

Mr. Welles stroked his beard, which is something he does when he is thinking. "Did you see it yourself?"

"Oh, yes, *sahib*. It has hair that grows all the way

down its back. Perhaps it changes into a wolf when the moon is at its fullest. This last, though, I have not yet seen, though my wife assures me it is so."

"Tell me, Chunarem, at what time does this man-ghost appear?" asked Mr. Welles. He took off his eye-glasses and cleaned them on his white linen handkerchief. He always carries one. Then he put the glasses on again, tucked the handkerchief securely into his jacket pocket, and stared at the villager quite intently with his piercing blue eyes. "Christ eyes," the villagers call them, being all dark-eyed themselves.

For a moment Chunarem looked as if he did not know whom to be more frightened of—the *manush-bagha* or the missionary. Then, summoning the last of his fading courage, he said, "It comes at dusk, Reverend *Sahib*. When the sun has gone out of the sky but still the soft light lingers."

Mr. Welles stroked his beard again. He was silent for a long time, the same silence that made all the younger children nervous. Abruptly he broke the silence. "Near the village?" he asked.

Chunarem was startled and jumped. Then he said, "About three miles away, sir. Through the forest. I saw it with the others when we went to gather firewood. Ordinarily the women and children would do such a thing, but there have been many wolves. . . ." His voice trailed off, indicating what the many wolves would do

**13**

with village women and their infants. Then, almost apologetically, he added, "It was my wife, *sahib*, who begged me to come to you, and the others agreed."

I had been sitting quietly in the corner through all this, taking notes in my book. I tried to be as quiet as possible, but at that very moment my pen slipped, squealing across the page and reminding Mr. Welles of my presence.

"Mohandas!" he barked. I stood up, and he sent me from the room. My wooden slippers made a great deal of noise on the den floor, but I was too proud and too afraid to slip them off. I was also too proud and too afraid to listen at the door, and so heard no more, but I could guess the rest.

The ghost worshipers were a silly people. They believed that a *manush-bagha* can go through the forest on trackless feet and come near a village at dusk to scream horribly. Since I now believed in the Christian god, as did we all at The Home, I was not afraid of such a ghost. And even if I was, of what consequence was it? The *manush-bagha* was in Godamuri, and I was in the outskirts of Midnapore, in a Christian orphanage where crosses guarded the doorposts of the brushwood fence so such a being could not enter.

An hour later, when the villager Chunarem had gone back to Godamuri, Mr. Welles called Rama and me into his study. His lady wife was there as well.

Usually I loved that study. It smelled of pipe smoke and leather. It had floor-to-ceiling bookshelves lined with volumes whose bindings were well-worn. As a reward, when one of us did especially well at lessons, Mr. Welles would let us borrow a book. The lowest three shelves held the ones we were allowed to read. So far I had read my way through *Pilgrim's Progress, The Water Babies,* and *A Christmas Carol.* I was just beginning *The Boy's King Arthur,* and I much admired the pictures, especially the one of Sir Launcelot as the wild man in the woods.

This time, however, I was not to be so happy, as Mr. Welles came right to the point without silences or prayers or a waterfall of words.

"I must go in the morning to Godamuri and see for myself what frightens the villagers so. They say it is a ghost, but we good Christians do not believe in them, do we?" He shook his head to offer us the answer.

Dutifully, first Rama and then I answered him back, head shake for head shake, though surely he knew that we Indians took that motion to mean either yes or no. And suddenly I was remembering the ghosts of Christmas past and present in the book I had just read. Was Mr. Dickens, I wondered, not a Christian man? Or perhaps those were particularly Christian ghosts and the ones we at The Home did not believe in were Hindu. Often I had such confusing thoughts, though Rama never did. He shook his head, but it meant that, ghosts or not, he was not afraid. To be afraid ahead of time one needs imagination.

"I want you two boys, who are the oldest in The Home and therefore almost of an age to leave us, to accompany me. The trip will take two nights and three days, although we will be gone from The Home much longer than that. I want the natives to see that two of their own kind—boys—are not afraid of so-called ghosts." He stroked his beard yet another time. "Be ready in the morning. Early."

We were dismissed, and Rama whispered to me, "But we are not of *their* kind," meaning the Santals. It was a distinction that meant a lot to him.

As we left, Mr. Welles was turning excitedly to his wife. "This, my dear," he said, "may at last be the miracle I have waited for so long. The reason that God has sent me to this place."

And she, in her ever-soft voice, replied, "Are not the children miracle enough, David?" adding as an afterthought, "Those poor boys. You have thoroughly frightened them, you know."

"Nonsense," he said.

In the hall I said to Rama, "Are we thoroughly frightened?"

"Of course not," he said. He squared his shoulders and smiled. "*Santals* are frightened, but we are not San-

16

tals." His smile grew broader under the beginnings of a mustache. He touched the mustache, preening the way he did each morning when he looked into the bit of mirror he had taken from Cook. "*I* am not frightened."

Not to be outdone or put in the same category as the wretched Santal villagers, I answered, "I am the same." It was a no-answer reply, but sufficient for Rama.

And that was how we were committed to courage on the road to Godamuri.

# THE ROAD TO GODAMURI

◆◆◆

WE LEFT THE NEAT RICE SWAMPS NEAR OUR ORPHANAGE EARLY
the next morning and traveled quickly into the barren
countryside that was crisscrossed with fast-flowing rivers. Herons stalked the shorelines, searching for frogs,
and I longed to watch them. All too soon we came into
the sal jungle, where I had never been before, the deep
jungle that is spread with a dense canopy of leaves and
vines.

Since Mr. Welles had traveled before to Godamuri,
there was a path of sorts already cut through this part
of the jungle. But the jungle is a living, breathing entity;

it is never still. Already creepers had rewoven most of the barriers from tree to tree.

I walked at the head of the bullock and tickled him under the chin to encourage him to pull the cart that was heavy with our supplies. He was lazy and loved the luxury of standing still, but he loved a chin tickle even more. Rama and the two carters swung axes against the new-grown foliage in our way. Mr. Welles would occasionally call out instructions from the cart, where he rode.

So thick with sal trees was this particular part of the jungle that it was shady even during the day. The sun might be overhead, but we were rarely able to see it through the green filtered light, until a single ray of sunshine would suddenly come through a rip in the fabric of leaves, reminding us that there was another world beyond and above the jungle. Dark as it was, it was not altogether gloomy, for the air was filled with the cries of rhesus monkeys and the steady *racheta-racheta* of the empty kerosene can fixed under the cart, with a protruding stick hitting against the wheels. The jungle was not even particularly frightening, for the noise of the stick did its job and scared away most of the wild beasts. And when one time we heard the cough of a big cat nearby and then, suddenly ahead of us, saw a tiger with her cubs, I reached into the cart behind Mr. Welles for the two tabor drums. Rama and I pounded on them, and the other men shouted, sending wave upon wave of noise into the air. The tiger vanished back into the black door of her cave, a bright red flash of meat in her mouth, and the cubs followed.

Often we saw peacocks perched on viny swings. And once, when we had stopped for lunch in one of the infrequent open places in the sal, Mr. Welles said to me, "Look carefully. Over there, Mohandas."

I looked and saw a herd of reddish-brown deer.

"They are Axis deer. *Axis axis*," Mr. Welles said. "Or as you natives call them, chital."

No sooner had he named them than they sprang up and ran off, leaving dust as thick as smoke behind.

"Chital," I repeated to myself as the cart started up once again and the sound of the stick against the wheels hid the sound of my mouthings. "Axis deer. *Axis axis*." For I was determined not to lose this gift of names. Later I would write it down in my book and so make it mine forever.

At night we slept under the cart, the four of us, and Mr. Welles slept in the cart. We kept a fire going at all times, encircling us, not for warmth but for protection against the night creatures of the jungle. One of the carters played a *narh*, and each evening before we settled down he would pull haunting music from the flute, a sound that seemed as much a part of the forest as the animal calls.

We all took turns with the fire, even Mr. Welles. He would dismount from the cart, where he slept guarding the medicine chest and the Bibles and the pamphlets about cleanliness and Christ.

And right after the playing of the *narh*, before we slept for the first round of the night, Mr. Welles would fire a shot from his big gun out past the fire. I wondered briefly out loud if he were aiming at ghosts, such things being ever present in my thoughts. But Rama, who had been on one or two trips before, said no.

"It is part of his religion, I think," said Rama, "for he calls on his god right before he pulls the trigger."

"*Our* god," I reminded him.

He gave that shake of the head somewhere between yes and no, and smiled, then moved away from me to the company of the two men.

I wrote all these things down in my book, which I kept under the drum in the cart. Once I caught Mr. Welles looking in my book. My scribblings must have puzzled him. It seemed for a moment as if he were going to ask me about them. After all, he had given me the book to improve my English writing, and my ciphers were not exactly what he had in mind. But then he did not ask, after all; he just stroked his beard and looked off into the distance at a ray of sunlight that had pierced the tight green lacings of sal.

It took two nights and three days to get to Godamuri, and all the time Mr. Welles pointed out the jungle to me. Some things he had learned from the Santal villagers in exchange for teaching them about the god he knew: how to clap hands in such a way as to call up the red jungle fowl, or how to tell time by watching the sal leaf wither. Other things he knew from books, such as the Latin names of the forest animals. He named in three different tongues each bird and creature we saw, and once he said to me, "A man has power over his world if he can name all the things in it, Mohandas. Just that way God has control over the world He made."

Mr. Welles never spoke in this way to Rama. But I do not think that Rama minded. He was always in front of the cart with the men, laughing and singing as they forced their sharp blades up and through the tangles of vines.

Two nights and three days—and not once did we talk about the reason for this particular trip, about the *manush-bagha* that screamed outside of Godamuri. But the nearer we got to its dwelling place, the more I could see it in the eye of my mind. By the time we had reached the outskirts of Godamuri, the *manush-bagha* I feared was as tall as Mr. Welles and laughed as it gnawed on Christian bones. I dreamed of it by day and night. And though I was too afraid of it to say its name aloud and so call it to me, anagrams of its name decorated the pages of my book. *Sham-bangs*, I called it. Or *bagman-hush*. A poor kind of magic.

The men of Godamuri rushed out to greet us through the green clumps of bamboo that hid the village. They had been warned of our arrival first by Chunarem the day before, and then by a charcoal burner, an old Santal man who lived a little way into the jungle. He had seen smoke from our second night's fire and had hurried to the village, shouting his discovery. Visitors were a rarity in Godamuri. The people of the village often went out to the regional *hâts*, the fairs, to sell things, but foreigners rarely came in.

The men washed our feet, which embarrassed me, but Rama whispered that the Santals do it to all strangers. And Mr. Welles reminded us that Christ himself washed the feet of his apostles. So I submitted to the custom but, I am afraid, with rather bad grace. Besides, I am extremely ticklish on the bottoms of my feet.

It was quite a processional back to the village itself, along the one main street of packed dirt that threaded between the adobe-and-thatch huts. Rama and the two carters, plus Chunarem and the twenty or so who had come to greet us, went along in front. I hung back near the cart. Then the bullock, suspecting the end of his journey, hurried forward for the first time, and I had to trot to keep up.

The village women, in white saris, with brass pitchers on their hips, came out to greet us. Mr. Welles blessed them all and dismounted from the cart. He lit his pipe. The smoke encircled his head like a halo.

At that, I fell behind the cart and entered the village last of all, following the trail of smoke from Mr. Welles' pipe, thinking about the *manush-bagha*, and being very afraid.

# VIEW FROM
# A MACHAN

◆◆◆

THE OTHERS STAYED UP LATE THAT NIGHT, DRINKING RICE
beer, reciting love poems, and boasting of what they
would do to the ghost. Only Mr. Welles and I retired
early, he to his prayers and I to a rice straw pallet on
the cold floor of Chunarem's house.

I did everything not to think about the coming morning: sums in my head, the words of hymns, a litany of
my chores at The Home, starting with emptying the
kitchen garbage and ending with cleaning the compound. I even spoke the names of all the children, their
family names and their pet names and the cruel nick-
names they each hated as well. But it was no use. All I

could think of was the ghost, and, thinking of this, I fell into a troubled sleep.

Rama shook me awake.

"Come," he said. "It is time."

We helped with the breakfast—woman's work at The Home—and then, packing another meal on our backs, we met Mr. Welles at the door of the cowshed. He was rubbing his hands together and looking pleased.

"They have built us a *machan* as I requested," he said. "We will watch this so-called ghost from there."

Though I had never been up on a *machan*, still I knew all about them. What boy of my age did not? The *machan* would be high above the place that the *manush-bagha* inhabited. And unlike tigers, ghosts do not climb trees. Yet I did not think it would be high enough, even then, for me to feel safe.

We went out boldly, Mr. Welles, Rama, and I, for it was our duty to show a good face to the Santals, who are but silly, frightened villagers. Chunarem was most reluctant to come, but Mr. Welles insisted that he had to show us the way. The rest of the Santals, even the ones who had boasted so loudly the night before, stayed behind. It was enough, they said, that they had built the *machan*. That had exhausted their courage. They did not want to return and further anger the ghost. This time we did not take the bullock and the cart, but our own carters came; they believed themselves well under the protection of Mr. Welles and his god.

Chunarem led us less than three miles from the village. His people pick a sal leaf and watch it turn brittle and in this way measure distances. It is not terribly accurate. Mr. Welles greatly preferred his pocket watch, and I agree. But the three miles Chunarem promised were foreshortened by the sal leaf. We went into the forest proper, past thick brakes of rattan and bamboo.

At last we came to a small clearing dominated by an ancient mohua tree, and Chunarem signaled us to stop. It was in that tree, its trunk crisscrossed with the marks of many bear claws, that the *machan* had been built at a height of fifteen feet. Mr. Welles rested his smoothbore against the tree and nodded silently, looking around. To one side of the clearing, near a stand of blackthorn, was a large termite mound. In that mound, according to the trembling Chunarem, lived the *manush-bagha*. It came out only at dusk and had been seen many times. He had seen it himself. Twice.

Though it was midmorning, still I feared going close to the mound, but on a sign from Mr. Welles, I joined him and Rama at its foot. Even with my heart beating wildly and tremors sliding up and down the insides of my legs, I did not dare disobey his direct command.

"Tell me what you see, Rama," Mr. Welles said.

Rama shrugged. "A white ant mound," he said. Then he smiled. It was a perfectly good answer, and he knew it, though he used no more words than were necessary.

"And you, Mohandas?"

Let loose by his command, my tongue clattered away. "A temple of dirt, sir, with a hollow door leading down," I said. Then, seeing the remains of a smaller, similar mound nearby, obviously destroyed by last year's rains, its secret, twisting passageways laid open to the sky, I added, "A central mound that is perhaps surrounded by smaller mounds that are like hallways between rooms."

"Good, keen observation. You should do likewise, Rama," Mr. Welles said.

Rama was not shamed by this. He smiled more broadly and shrugged, as if to say he had seen the same and not thought it worth mentioning.

Mr. Welles continued. "Do either of you think a ghost could—or would—inhabit such a place?"

Chunarem answered quickly, "But it does, *sahib*. I have seen it."

"You have seen something," agreed Mr. Welles. Then he turned and looked directly at me. "Mohandas?"

My wide-open eyes were my only answer.

"Never mind," said Mr. Welles. "We will see at dusk what this ghost of Godamuri really is."

"You will shoot it, *sahib?*" asked Chunarem, gesturing toward the smoothbore leaning against the fig tree. "You will kill it?"

Mr. Welles pulled out his pipe, lit it, and laughed. "If

it is a ghost," he said, "then I doubt a gun could kill it, for it is not alive. But anything else will fall to my shot."

"But it *is* a ghost," Chunarem argued.

Mr. Welles laughed again and pointed at the ground around the mound with his walking stick. "A ghost with wolf feet," he said, "is no ghost that I recognize. But certainly one I might shoot." He reached out and patted Chunarem on the shoulder. "Do not worry. By tonight this ghost will be explained."

I did not understand that exchange at all, but was thankful at last when we were allowed to leave the mound and make our way to the other side of the clearing, under the mantle of the fig. There we spread a cloth and ate our luncheon in silence. I kept my back against the tree, having checked it first for snakes.

Frequently Mr. Welles stood up and walked back to look around the clearing, poking at things with a stick and leaving a trail of pipe smoke to mark his passage. Chunarem began a long, pointless story about a village festival, which Rama and the carters seemed to enjoy. I drew pictures in my book of Mr. Welles' smoke as it hovered over the mound. In the drawing the smoke looked like a ghost. I surrounded the picture with a border of crosses.

Above us in a tree a colony of langurs, their tails curved above their backs like question marks, scolded and warned of intruders. Then at last, wearying of their inattentive audience, they moved off, leaping from branch to branch until they disappeared into the jungle canopy.

Long before the sun started down, we climbed the rope ladder on the blind side of the mohua tree up to the *machan*. I pulled the ladder up after us. Chunarem recited the *Pujas* before going back to the village, rather thankful to quit the place, and our two carters went with him to feed the bullock. It was just the three of us in the tree. Mr. Welles put his pipe away and cocked his gun. We waited.

Almost an hour went by. Shadows began to creep into the clearing. A slight breeze stirred the leaves. We did not move, not even to slap away the mosquitoes. I was lulled into a half sleep by the cicada hum and the infrequent low call of the green fruit pigeons as they settled down for the night.

Then, all of a sudden, out of the main entrance to the mound, which was partially hidden by a plum bush, came a full-grown wolf, its ears back, head up, sniffing. It was soon followed by another, and then a third close on its heels. They came drawn out together in a graceful motion, sniffing in unison. After them came two small cubs. They were all a kind of indistinct gray-brown, with white stomachs and the sloping hindquarters of a jackal. The first wolf turned, and the others half lay down before her, wagging their tails, cowed by her great pale yellow eyes.

And then the ghost emerged.

Hand and foot, it was like a human being, just as Chunarem had said. Its enormous head was covered with hair as alive as a nest of snakes, and a sharp, pointed light-brown muzzle of a face peered out of the nest. It looked around once, twice, then ran on all fours with a quick, crablike gait and lay down next to the mother wolf.

The *manush-bagha* was clearly not itself a wolf, for it had a covering of that horrible hair only from its head to halfway down its body. It had no tail, and its legs were long with jointed knees. It ran more like a scuffling squirrel than with the long, eager lopings of a wolf. Once it raised its head up toward the *machan*, and I held my breath in fear that it would notice me. I could see its bright eyes. They were dark, piercing, and inhuman.

Suddenly a second ghost, exactly like the first, only much smaller, came out of the hole. It rubbed against the mother wolf and against the other ghost, then it reached out for the wolf's ear with one grubby paw.

"Shoot!" croaked Rama.

Mr. Welles raised the gun, then lowered it slowly and shook his head.

I looked down to see what it was he saw.

At Rama's voice, the wolves and the *manush-baghas* had disappeared into the ever-darkening forest. The clearing was full of shadows and nothing more.

*31*

We climbed down from the *machan* and, without speaking, returned to Godamuri. I looked only at the path beneath my feet the entire way, afraid and yet strangely thankful that we had not shot the ghosts, but more thankful still that we arrived safely in that ugly little village alive enough to drink cup after cup of their famous rice beer and to beat the drums that marked the meeting of the missionary and the *manush-bagha*.

# CATCHING A
# GHOST

♦♦♦

IN THE MORNING MY HEAD FELT SWOLLEN, AND MY THROAT
ached, and I swore that I would never again drink rice
beer. I remembered little of the night, but Mr. Welles
greeted me with the same stern courtesy he always gave
to Rama, not the gentler inviting tones he normally used
with me. It was as if he placed me in a different category
now that I had gone out carousing with the village men.
I did not like it and wondered if I had said or done
something foolish in his hearing, but surely Rama would
have commented on it.

It was only after I splashed water on my face that I
recalled our mission for the day. We were to capture

the *manush-baghas*, bringing one or both back.

The plan, as Mr. Welles had explained it, was quite simple.

"We will take my twenty-bore, our camp kit, the great winding sheets the Santals call *gelaps*, and my field glasses," he said. "The carters will each have a rifle, and you boys each a shovel. The village men will accompany us and beat the bushes, raising a shout from afar. They are too terrified, poor heathen, to come closer." He looked straight at Rama. "We must show them how brave a Christian can be."

Rama could not meet his eyes, and I recalled Rama's frightened shout.

But whether or not Rama was still frightened, I was infected with fear as great as or greater than that of any heathen. My body was rashed with it. I shuffled my feet.

Rama looked over and smiled for the first time that day, as if my fear excused his.

"We will be brave, sir," he said, placing an elbow expertly in my ribs.

I coughed. "Unlike the Santals, sir," I added.

"Good boys," Mr. Welles said.

At first Rama and I walked with the beaters, tramping so loudly through the bushes that the noise drove both animals and fear before us. The *sakwa* sounded every so often, and at each horn blow we raised a shout anew.

Several small hares started at our feet. I pretended my fear was fastened to the shoulder of one particular hare whose left ear was splashed with white. As it dashed into the undergrowth, I could almost feel my terror disappear with it.

But then an older man, speaking to Chunarem, who was reluctantly with us, said, "I have faced unarmed the charge of a tiger and lived. I would do that again rather than face this ghost."

At his words the hare loosed my fear, and it bounded back to me, seeming to stay in my throat. I could hardly swallow. So I went back from the line of beaters to walk by Mr. Welles' side, comforted by his presence and the big twenty-bore gun he carried.

Up ahead of us the scattered line of men kept walking between the trees. Their white loincloths were stray patches of light in the shadowy jungle. It was like some kind of ritual dance, with the *sakwa* accompaniment. I was both part of it and apart from it, concentrating on my own steps. The three miles that day were every bit as long as the withering leaf foretold, yet we came at last to the clearing.

The villagers did not proceed in but waited in a ragged circle some fifty yards back. Mr. Welles plunged through them, and I, drawn to his side by my thread of fear, followed. So we were the first to reach the mound. Then came Rama and, last, the two carters, their guns already on their shoulders.

"Dig," said Mr. Welles, nodding his head toward the ant mound.

Rama began. After a long moment I put my shovel into the dirt.

The mound was packed hard by the last rains, and it did not crumble easily. We had to attack it fiercely, and it continued to resist us. I dug steadily near the bush, filling in the hole as much as hollowing it out. Rama hacked away at the other entrance. Mr. Welles, with his rifle on his shoulder, stood guard.

For a time the only sound in the clearing was the smack of shovel against dirt and the intake of breath on each upswing.

Suddenly two of the wolves exploded out of a hidden side entrance, close to the spot where the beaters waited warily. The line of men broke apart, and the wolves ran past them, disappearing quickly into the brush.

I was watching the confusion when something hairy brushed past my arm. I tried to cry out and could not. Fearfully I looked down. It was the mother wolf, her ears flattened and her teeth bared, growling. She ran straight toward the carters. One of them shot at her but in his haste aimed wide and nearly hit me. The second carter shot with care and struck her once high on the shoulder, and after she fell, a second time in the chest.

*36*

She screamed, a cry so like that of a human that it pierced my heart.

She died slowly, crying and shuddering every so often and then finally guttering out like a candle.

We watched her agonies silently, unable to do anything for her. Mr. Welles knelt down by her head and touched her gently. The carters congratulated one another with nods and grins, and the villagers kept back, once again in a line.

And still there was no sign of the *manush-bagha*.

Mr. Welles stood up. "Dig!" he said, his voice breaking slightly.

Rama and I began to dig, quickly now. Rama attacked the main door, which crumbled at last in such a way that the central cave was laid open to the sky.

Inside the hollow we saw the strangest sight. The two cubs and two hideous creatures—the *manush-baghas*—were huddled together in a monkey ball. Their arms and legs were clutched around each other, and it was hard to tell where one began and the other ended. They would not look up, and the ball shook as if they were horribly afraid. All of a sudden my own fear melted away, and all I felt was a profound sadness, like an empty place, in my chest.

Mr. Welles put his rifle down and leaned over the mound. "Come," he called. "We must bring them up separately." He put his hand into the monkey ball, using the other hand to prize them apart.

"Damnation!" he cried suddenly, the greatest oath I had ever heard him mutter. He stood up and showed us his hand. The smaller ghost had bitten him, ripping the tender skin between his thumb and forefinger. He held the hand against his shirt to stanch the wound.

"Rama, get me the four *gelaps*," he said.

Rama threw the shovel to one side and went to the line of villagers to collect the big sheets. I took the time to lean over the mound.

"Why," I said, my voice returning to me, though only in a whisper, "they are not ghosts but human beings."

Mr. Welles put his hand to his chin, musing. "Children, Mohandas, probably outcasts from a village, raised by wolves. And we have just killed the only mother they remember." He turned to look for Rama, who was taking a very long time collecting the sheets.

I thought about that for a moment. Children of the wolf. They were orphans, just as I was, alone and afraid. Into the hollow I whispered, "I am your brother."

One cub looked up at me, but the wolf-children did not. They clutched their litter mates and howled, the sound of an animal in deep distress.

Rama returned at last, one section of cloth trailing behind him, and dumped the wrappings on the ground at Mr. Welles' feet. He smiled broadly but said nothing.

Mr. Welles gathered up one sheet and threw it over the monkey ball, obscuring the four. Rama leaped into the tiny pit and secured the wrapping. Then Mr. Welles leaned over and, aided by the two carters, lifted the trembling bundle out of the mound.

By this time the villagers had gathered enough courage to approach the wolf den, chattering like children at a *hât*, laughing and shoving until Mr. Welles stopped them.

"Hush!" he said. "Do not frighten the poor little things with your foolishness."

"But, *sahib*," said Chunarem, "they have already given us many weeks of fright. Now it is our turn."

The other men cheered at his words, but Mr. Welles gave them such a look that they quieted at once.

Still, brave as their words were, the villagers did not want to touch the squirming bundle. Rama and I, with Mr. Welles' help, undid the wrapping carefully and slipped out first one and then the other of the cubs, tying each up in an individual *gelap*. Apart, they were as like puppies as anything else.

I was the one who prized apart the two wolf-children, which is how I knew, before anyone else, that they were both girls, thin and knobby and wild. The little one was so small that my hand could slip around her upper arm, and still one could see space where my finger touched my thumb.

"It is all right," I crooned to them, using the same low tones I adopted with the baby animals at The Home.

The smaller one relaxed. But long after I had gotten the larger one tied up, with the help of Mr. Welles, she glared fiercely around and snarled at us, her captors. Only when she looked at me, I imagined a kind of recognition, orphan to orphan, as we were both afraid and alone in an alien world.

# TWO CAGES

### ◆◆◆

THE TRIP BACK TO GODAMURI WAS A STRANGE PROCESSIONAL.
Each carter carried one of the wolf-girls, wrapped securely in a *gelap*, over his shoulder like a sack of rice.
The Santals traded back and forth with the wolf cubs,
which they had freed from the sheets. The cubs were
no longer afraid of the men and licked their hands and
faces with eager pink tongues. Indeed, the cubs seemed
to have forgotten what had happened to their mother.

Rama petted each cub in turn, laughing loudly, but I
noticed he was careful to keep his back to the wolf-
children, as if ignoring them restored his former courage
completely.

Mr. Welles walked by himself, smoking his pipe, lost in thought.

Every once in a while one of the villagers would hang back and examine the captives, bravely poking with the butt of a bamboo spear at the restrained bodies. The wolf-children let out no more than a few snarls at the treatment, though once the smaller one snapped at the carter's hand. Then she suddenly lapsed into a comalike sleep from which no amount of poking seemed to waken her.

At last I could stand no more.

"Such brave men!" I shouted as one Santal pushed the bamboo into the backside of the larger wolf-child. "And where were you, so brave, when they were unbound and in their den?"

He looked at me uncomprehendingly. "But that was when we thought they were *manush-baghas*," he said.

Another added, "Now we know they are *bhuts*, spirits of children who died before initiation. They are outcasts who must wander the forest and prey on mortals. But they can be killed, and that is what we shall do when we return to Godamuri."

"No!" I screamed, and pushed at the man who spoke, trying to wound him with my fists and feet.

Arms came around me, and the smell of smoke enveloped me, causing me to cough.

"No, indeed," Mr. Welles' voice said from above my head. "The boy is right. These are not evil spirits of

yours. They are a miracle sent to test *me*. You shall
see—I will tame these little devils, and they will become
human again. Will that not prove to you that Christ is
the one God?"

The Santals backed away from him, trying to understand what he was saying. He continued to hold me and
calm me with a waterfall of words, all the while standing
us between the villagers and the carters, who held their
prey.

And so we returned to Godamuri with only Mr. Welles'
words between the wolf-children and disaster. His in-
tuition told him that it would be too dangerous to remain in the village overnight should the men celebrate
the capture of the *bhuts* with too much rice beer. Ordinarily the Santals are a harmless people, gentle and
not easily angered, but fear makes a man do peculiar
things.

"We will return to The Home at once," Mr. Welles
advised us. Then he bargained for two cages with Chunarem, paying with a sack of tobacco and several bags
of rice, even though he knew the villagers would get a
good price at a *hât* for the cubs, and so he really owed
them nothing.

The little captives, now smelling of stale urine and
sweat, lay unbound inside the locked cages. We lifted
the cages onto the cart. Our bullock strained to pull the
load and would have balked, but I tickled him under

the chin, which reminded him of home, and as though he suddenly smelled the luxury of his own shed ahead, he went all the rest of the way through the jungle contentedly.

We saw nothing in the jungle larger than a langur on the road home, though the jungle itself seemed darker. The tight lacings of the sal canopy let in little light, and there were continual distant rumblings of thunder, though the rains were long past.

I tried to feed the bigger wolf-girl cow's milk from a spoon whenever we stopped. When she turned her head away, I asked Mr. Welles to let me use his handkerchief. He offered it with a puzzled look on his face, but asked no questions. I tore the handkerchief up and rolled the smaller portions into wicks, which I dipped into the cup of milk. When a wick was soaking wet, I put one end into the wolf-girl's mouth, letting the other end remain in the cup. She began sucking on the wet wick as if it were a teat, and so she took nourishment eagerly, though she would not look straight at me while she did it.

The little one, though, refused to eat, and I worried about that. She was so thin already that her ribs were like the vaultings of a cathedral I had seen in one of Mr. Welles' books. And her breathing was labored. But each time I offered her a wick, her lips pulled back from her teeth, and she growled at me like a wolf. I kept talking to her gently through the bars of her cage, and I tried to get her to eat. Twice I left a cup of milk with the wick in it overnight, but both mornings the milk was spilled out and the floor of the cage was covered with flies.

They slept most of the day but lay awake and alert at night. When we took turns at the watch, Rama would not go near the cart, preferring to sit by the fire, but I could not keep away from the cages, checking them frequently to see that everything was all right.

Each time I looked, the larger wolf-girl stared back at me, her round eyes shining with a peculiar blue glare. Only in the jungle had I ever seen such eyes, the eyes of the beasts peering from the underbrush. I said nothing of it to the others, though I wrote it down in my book.

And so we returned after two nights and three days to The Home, disheveled and quite dirty ourselves. We were relieved to get back to civilization.

When we started to unload the cart in the courtyard, Mrs. Welles and the children ran out, making a wide, ragged circle around the cages.

Krithi stared thoughtfully at the wolf-girls and put his finger in his mouth, a sure sign that he was unhappy. Veda, after one quick glance, ran to the sanctuary of Mrs. Welles' skirts. She was followed by the other littler ones, though Preeti, in her own peculiar manner, turned sideways once to look at them. But Indira watched it all with a kind of pleased expression on her face.

Mr. Welles helped supervise the unloading of the cages, then turned to his wife.

"These poor mites were what those heathen mistook for ghosts," he said. "Cleaned up, with good, sensible haircuts, they will be indistinguishable from our other children. One seems about three years old, the other nine or ten. We will eventually get them to tell us all about their lives with the wolves. God is good, my dear. I shall have something very special to report about His work and ours to the bishop now." He smiled in a self-satisfied way.

But Mrs. Welles shook the little ones from her skirts and ran over and knelt before the cages, shielding what was inside from our eyes.

"They are girls, David, girls. And the biggest must be nearing puberty. How could you expose them in this manner? How could you cage them in this inhuman way? Quick, Veda, Indira." She gave orders in a quiet voice that brooked no arguments. "Find me clothing that will fit these two. A shift will do for each. And some cloth for diapers until they can be taught rudimentary manners. Poor things." She stood up, holding her skirts out as curtains, guarding them. "A miracle, Mr. Welles? It will be a miracle if they have not been violated, running around the forest without a stitch of clothing on. We must send for the doctor."

As Indira and Veda returned with the cotton shifts, I saw Rama smile behind his hand at the two carters. And it came to me suddenly that he had certainly noticed that the wolf-children were girls before now, just as I had, though there seemed something sly and mocking and knowing in his look.

Krithi, Preeti, and the little ones were bustled off by Cook to do their chores and studies, laughing and glancing back over their shoulders at Veda and Indira, who circled the cages warily. They held the clothing in their hands, not quite sure what to do with it, fearing they might be savaged at any minute by the wolf-girls in the cages.

Mr. and Mrs. Welles stood apart, watching them.

Suddenly I was ashamed, ashamed for all of us. For Rama and his smirking manhood. For Mr. Welles and his ugly little miracle. For Mrs. Welles and her need for clean, concealing clothes. For Indira and Veda and the rest, who had not welcomed these new children into The Home.

But most of all I was ashamed that the little wolf-girls, who had done no one any harm and who had been living out their lives as uncomplaining and unthinking as the animals in the jungle, should have been brought here to be civilized against their wills. And I, who had also been abandoned at The Home, had been powerless to stop it.

# FIRST DAY

## ♦♦♦

BECAUSE THEY WERE GIRLS AND HAD TO BE BATHED, I SAW no more of them that day. But Indira told us about it later, and what a feast she had in the telling. She waited until we were all done with supper and had our free time outdoors. Then she began.

"They smell, you know."

The little ones nodded.

I thought it stupid to reply, keeping to myself the fact that any of us, similarly treated, would smell as bad.

"And their bodies were so dirty," she reported. "Layers upon layers. Mrs. Welles said they would have to be soaked for days to get it all off. And they scratch as if they were dogs."

"Fleas," whispered Veda.

"Fleas," the little ones responded.

Of course we all know that many of the villagers have fleas. And lice. We do not. The English do not allow it.

"And did they like the bath?" asked Krithi, his finger hovering near his mouth.

"Like it? They loathed it," replied Indira with a wicked-sounding laugh. "In the end we had to throw buckets of water over them while Mrs. Welles held first one and then the other. She never did get them clean, though she herself was quite soaked."

The idea of Mrs. Welles being wet made us all laugh with Indira. Actually, we all liked Mrs. Welles, the little ones often quarreling over whose turn it was to sit in her lap during evening stories. But to think of her dripping—her hair, usually so tidy and pinned, plastered down over her ears with water—was really funny. I joined the laughter.

Indira pantomimed it well, and our laughter further encouraged her. She grabbed Rama around the waist, pretending she was washing him. He screamed in a high-pitched voice, half words, half howls.

"Oh, no! A-woooooo!" he cried.

That started us all laughing again.

Suddenly Indira let Rama go. "But you should have seen the scars," she said.

"Scars," Veda whispered.

"Scars," Preeti echoed.

"What scars?" I asked.

Indira turned to me and said, "When some of the dirt was removed, we could see their bodies were covered with scars. And scratches. And scabs. It was quite horrible." She shuddered.

Veda nodded and whispered, "And their knees. Tell about their knees."

Eagerly we all turned to Indira.

"Their knees—and their hands and elbows, too—have these heavy pads of flesh on them."

"Calluses," I said.

"Horrible," Indira added.

We were silent at the thought. Then I said, in the most sensible and calming voice I could manage, "From running on all fours, of course. That's what those calluses are. From running on hands and knees. Nothing more."

"On all fours!" Indira's voice was full of scorn. "Like an animal!"

Rama smiled. "They think they are wolves," he said in Bengali. He got down on his hands and knees and made playful, growling passes at Veda. Indira shoved

Veda aside and got down on her own hands and knees, growling back at him.

"Actually," I began, remembering that first night when they had disappeared into the sal, "they can run very fast that way. Faster than a man can run upright." But no one heard me. They were all too busy laughing at Rama and Indira, who were playing at being wolves.

I stopped talking and went over to the garden wall, staring at the wall and at the lantana bushes without really seeing them. But the sound of Rama's play snarls and Indira's shrieking laughter followed me.

That night at our prayers Mr. Welles spoke very forcefully to us.

"My children," he said, "our little miracles have been cleaned up and are safe within the compound walls, but they are, as yet, unused to the company of human beings. This is to be expected. Therefore tonight—and for the next few nights if needed—they will sleep outside in the courtyard with the dogs. Do not disturb them. Do not frighten them. Treat them with Christian kindness. Soon they will reward us with tales of the jungle and stories of wonders such as mankind rarely beholds."

With that, he blessed us and sent us off to bed.

Rama fell asleep at once, but I lay restless for many hours. At last I got up and looked out the window. I could see the brushwood wall of the compound, bleached by the full moon. It was the very edge of my comfortable universe.

Then I heard a whining sound, like that made by a puppy newly taken from its littermates. After the whine came a kind of snuffling whimper.

I knew it was the wolf-children.

Rama was still snoring lightly, and I did not waken him. On the nights when he stayed home, he slept like a lump until dawn.

I climbed out the window and dropped to the ground, turning my ankle slightly.

The whimpers stopped at once, but I was able to follow the memory of that sound to the place where two walls made a corner. There, curled around each other, were the wolf-girls. Snuggled against them were three puppies who, when they noticed me, looked up and wagged their tails.

At my approach, the younger wolf-girl lifted her head and stared past me. Her wide night-shining eyes glinted with blue lights. She growled.

The larger girl put her head back and howled, baying at the bright orb of the moon. The sound lifted the hairs on the back of my neck, and I wanted to cry.

"There, there," I muttered. "Hush, now, hush."

My crooning efforts made no difference. She howled once more.

I moved closer, despite the snarl of the younger girl, and put my hand out to them.

It must have been the motion that stopped a third howl. The older girl turned toward me. I could see the shape of her head clearly now. Without that huge ball of snarled hair, she seemed smaller, more vulnerable.

"There, there," I said again. Then I pointed to myself, saying in the most persuasive voice I could manage, "I am your friend, Mohandas. Friend. Mohandas."

The little one did not growl again, but rather put her head down on her hands and feigned a sleepy indifference. The big one looked at me once more, scratched quickly behind her right ear, then turned away. Like an animal, she could not bear a human's eyes upon her.

"I am Mohandas," I said once again. "What are your names?"

But then she, too, lay down to sleep.

I stood slowly and when neither of them moved again, I returned to the window. At least I had quieted them. That much was easy. I had a harder time getting back in the window.

Just before dropping off to sleep, I realized that it had been I, not Rama, who had slipped in and out without being caught. The thought of *that* made me smile, and I must have been smiling, still, when I fell asleep.

# TROUBLES

♦♦♦

TROUBLE BEGAN ALMOST AT ONCE. IN THE MORNING WE SAW that the wolf-girls had torn off their shifts and ripped them to shreds. Little pieces of the clothing were found all over the compound. While Mrs. Welles tried matter-of-factly to put new dresses on them, Indira started pinching the younger children. Preeti stood with her back to the compound wall, head tilted, trying to see what all the excitement was about. And Veda gave up talking altogether in favor of periodic screams.

Mr. Welles, who usually spent mornings in his study working on parish business, came out and tried to quiet everyone down, but he was clearly ill at ease and got in the way.

Rama, looking at Krithi, who was sucking his finger and half a fist as well, muttered, "They have brought evil here."

I turned to Mr. Welles. "Sir, could such a thing be so?"

"Nonsense," he growled. "Rama, Mohandas, I am surprised at you. Such a notion is a heathen notion. I thought we had taught you better. It is just that these poor girls disturb us. They are, in ways both subtle and unsubtle, not quite human—yet. And we all find that unsettling. But evil? Nonsense. In a little while we will all look back at today and laugh at it. 'A day of troubles,' we will say. Now run along and do your homework."

"Words," muttered Rama in Bengali. "You will see. They are *bhuts* and evil. No amount of words will change that."

But they did not look evil to me, just pathetic. And so very alone.

Before the noon meal Cook had threatened to quit. Though the day maids and the carters had all, in their turn, threatened to quit many times that I knew of, this was the first time for Cook. She was loyal, possibly, Indira had suggested once, because she was such a bad cook that no one else would have her.

"They are filthy beasts," Cook shrieked at Mrs. Welles. The trouble, it seemed, was that the wolf-girls had used one of the day's quieter moments to steal an uncooked, unplucked chicken from the pantry window. The two of them had shared their catch with the dogs, eating the chicken raw and rubbing the bones on the ground to separate the meat. The smaller wolf-girl still had feathers and particles of meat on her lips.

"Beasts!" Cook screamed once more, which started Veda shrieking all over again.

The wolf-girls responded by howling, and Indira smiled, looking radiant. Trouble was definitely her element.

Mr. Welles came out of his study and stood in the arched doorway. His face was purple. He took off his glasses and cleaned them quite thoroughly with his handkerchief, a gesture that took enough time to calm everyone down. Then he listened to Cook's complaint and sighed loudly, a sound I had never heard from him before.

"Rama, get the bones away from them," he ordered. "You know that chicken bones could choke the dogs."

Rama went outside at once, almost grateful to be away from the shrieking women, though he was less than eager to go near the wolf-girls.

Mr. Welles turned to me. "And now, Mohandas, tell me why you are smiling."

It was true. My grin spread broadly. I was absurdly pleased. "Because they are eating, sir. Real food. Not just a bit of milk sucked up from a handkerchief wick."

Mr. Welles looked down at the handkerchief, which he still held in his left hand. He folded it slowly, carefully, and put it back in his coat pocket.

"Quite so," he said at last. "You are right, Mohandas." He turned to his wife and Cook. "Mohandas has put his finger on it. The girls are eating. *Eating.* Let us give thanks."

Cook scowled, ready to give another shriek instead, but Mrs. Welles cast a strange, unreadable look at her husband, then clicked her tongue at Cook. We all folded our hands and were preparing to offer thanks for the wolf-girls' appetites—and the momentary peace—when there came an awful scream from outside, the sound of a slap, and then some truly terrible cursing in Bengali.

Rama ran in. "She bit me. *Bit* me!" he said, first in Bengali, then in English. Blood coursed down his palm. "And now they are eating dirt."

Mrs. Welles turned quickly. "Indira, you get me the bandages. You, Veda, the carbolic. Really, David, what will we do if sepsis sets in? They may be rabid, you know. It's already clear they have fleas."

"They are hardly rabid, my dear. I was bitten myself and nothing happened. And wild animals often eat pebbles and sand after a meal." His words seemed to bring her little comfort, and she bustled about with twice the movement necessary as a kind of signal of her anger and concern.

Rama gritted his teeth when she cleansed his hand and poured the carbolic on the wound.

And that was only the morning.

In the afternoon Mrs. Welles attempted giving the wolf-girls another bath and hair washing, and this time was more successful. She used the strongest soap—the carbolic soap—and then noticed that the smaller girl was developing sores on her legs, strange granulations that were eating away at the hard calluses on her knees. I helped by holding each of the girls in turn, for Rama would not go near them again, and Indira, Preeti, and Veda were much too weak for the task. Only when Mrs. Welles bathed their private parts, under the loincloths, did I have to look away.

Mrs. Welles dosed the little one's sores with boric acid and zinc oxide and bandaged the worst places with cotton. But the wolf-girl never made a sound all the while Mrs. Welles touched the wounds. It was as if she did not know how to cry.

When the other children came into the courtyard to play, they stood in a large circle around the wolf-girls.

"Look!" Indira said in that overbright voice I had come to distrust. "She's a leper. Leper, leper!" she cried.

The other children were quick to pick up her words. "Leper, leper," they aped back.

Only Rama, who stood with a shoulder against the wall, and I were outside the circle and silent. He because he pretended to be above childish things, and I because I hated such games. Eventually Rama made a face and left, but I did not. It was as though I were paralyzed, unable to stop the teasing but equally unable to stop watching.

"No nose, no nose," Indira called out, and the others echoed her.

Suddenly Indira broke into the circle and pinched the little wolf-girl's leg, above the bandaged knee.

The wolf-girl, who had been so silent under Mrs. Welles' painful ministrations, howled. The larger wolf-child rushed at Indira, running on all fours, and clawed her arm badly. Although she drew no blood, there were four streak marks from elbow to wrist that remained red welts for most of the day.

Indira screamed and ran from the courtyard, back into the building, the other children at her heels.

The wolf-girl did not chase after them but crawled slowly over to the door. She raised her head and sniffed the air. Then she swiveled and stared toward me.

I looked around carefully. I was the only one left outside.

I could feel my heart thudding under my cotton shirt,

and I put my hands out slowly to show her I meant no harm. Fear drove me to begin speaking in the same quiet tones I had used with her the night before.

"See, see, I will not hurt you. See, see, do not be afraid."

She stood uncertainly, moving her head back and forth in a peculiar swaying motion, and, emboldened, I edged toward her.

"I—will—not—hurt—you," I said again, stopping some ten paces away. Then I pointed to myself, my hand shaking slightly. "Mohandas. I am Mohandas. What is your name?"

She did not answer.

"What is your name?" I asked again.

Her silence was complete. It was as though she had no tongue at all.

"I will call you . . . Kamala," I said, my tongue chattering away. "That means lotus. And your sister, Amala, bright yellow flower. Pretty names. Kamala. Amala. Do you like the sound of those names?"

She looked down and turned from me, going back to the little wolf-girl. She nudged Amala with her head, and the two of them made their slow way back to the place where the walls came together in a corner. They crowded into it and sat, huddled. Kamala circled three times on her hands and knees, then lay down, head on hands. Amala sat and picked forlornly at the bandages, slowly shredding them. Soon there was a pile of white cotton pieces by her side. She faced the corner the whole while.

"Kamala," I whispered. "Amala."

But if they heard me, if they understood at all, they made no sign.

# AMALA AND
# KAMALA

♦♦♦

WE HAD REACHED A KIND OF CAUTIOUS TRUCE WITH THE
wolf-girls. Indira and the others stayed as far away as
possible, and when circumstances forced them to cross
the wolf-children's paths, they made a sign with two
fingers to ward away evil. Rama walked by them as
stiffly as a drill sergeant and as far as his pride would
admit. A growl, a lifted lip, or a snarl was enough to
send any of the younger children screaming back into
the house. Krithi took to carrying a large stick whenever he went out.

A scream or a shout or a gesture with the stick would
make the wolf-girls scamper back to their corner. There

they would snuggle into a monkey ball, uncurling instantly if one of us violated what they considered their home ground.

It was one step forward and then retreat for the better part of the week, and by week's end it was difficult to say which of us was ahead. Even Mrs. Welles could not get close to them without threats. She had to resort to throwing buckets of water at them to clean them off.

Eventually Amala picked off all her bandages. It surprised us to see that the wounds underneath had healed.

Only at night, under cover of darkness, could I still manage to maneuver close to them. Not that they were unaware of me then. With their shining night eyes and uncanny hearing, they knew I was on my way as soon as my leg was over the window ledge. Although I could see them only as shadowy figures at night, I was convinced that they could see me as well in the dark as they did in the daylight, and it seemed that nighttime lent permission to our uneasy friendship.

One night Rama saw me climbing over the sill.

"Where are you going?" he asked. "Out to Tantigoria? Wait, I will go with you. It has been weeks since I have gone. My mouth aches for rice beer and the talk of men."

I shook my head but did not answer, only looked away from him.

And then he knew. For a moment he said nothing,

then in Bengali he spat out, "They are evil."

"They are children," I answered, "even as you and I."

"No!" he said fiercely.

"Look at them, Rama," I begged. "They have arms and legs and faces and bodies like ours."

"Do not compare me with those—those things."

*Things.* Neither beast nor human. In a way it was true. By day they were such a sorry lot, and I think somehow they sensed it. That was why they preferred the darkness. In the direct sun they always breathed harder and sought out the shadowed corners to hide in. Fire of any kind made them whimper with fear. Even a lit match threw them into paroxysms of anxiety. I never, after that first night when they were caged, used my kerosene lamp.

It was in the daytime that their physical differences were obvious. Their arms and hands were longer than ours, reaching almost to their knees. The nails of their fingers were worn on the inside and strangely rounded. Mr. Welles surmised that was due to all their scratching and scrabbling in the dirt.

Their feet were peculiar as well, the big toes longer and somewhat crooked, making an angle when they stood flat-footed on the ground. Almost ape foot, Indira said, not like a proper wolf foot. And when they stood up, their feet rested wholly on the ground with no visible arch, the toes spread out to support their weight.

They walked on hands and feet, not like a human at all. Forced upright, they teetered painfully, dropping back to all fours as soon as possible. I wrote a sketch of them in my book and tried to walk that way myself. After a minute it hurt my back and strained my thighs, yet Amala and Kamala ran quickly in this manner, scuttling across the courtyard when they played with the dogs.

It was their faces that were the strangest of all, and the most frightening, for it was there that they seemed the most removed from humanity: eyes set in two hollows, thin, long noses ending in two wide nostrils, and the nostrils themselves able to widen and flare as easily as a dog's. Their eyeteeth were longer and more pointed than normal.

Rama called them ugly. "Pig ugly," he said.

Yet I saw a strange, perverse beauty in their faces, a look that hovered somewhere between the human and the beast.

After the first week they ate from a plate, more in imitation of the puppies than the people. They lowered their mouths to lap at bowls placed on the ground. It appalled Cook, but they still preferred their meat raw or at least undercooked. If given a bowl of rice and vegetables and meat, they would nose out the meat and leave the rest. So Mrs. Welles insisted that, for a while at least, they be catered to, although Mr. Welles worried that a diet of near-raw meat would keep their tempers inflamed.

"They will be dead in a week if they do not eat," said Mrs. Welles sensibly, and so it was settled.

Since Cook threatened, halfheartedly, to leave rather than serve meat raw (she preferred burning the food, said Indira), Mrs. Welles sighed and took on the job herself.

"We must slowly accustom them to being human," she explained to us all. That was at dinner, right after Krithi had found them eating and rolling in the half-picked carcass of a wood pigeon that had flown over the compound wall in the night.

Mr. Welles saw his duty differently. He would first teach them to speak and then to be Christians. He enlisted me as his chief helper.

"Mohandas," he said as I stood uneasily waiting to be informed of my new duties. "Without the Word, they will remain beasts. And though the Lord loves the beasts of the fields and forests, He prefers human beings, for He made us—and not them—in His image."

Still I waited.

"You will be let off all other chores and tend only to the wolf-children. Tame them. Accustom them to your sight and smell. Then begin to teach them words. Simple words at first. Me. You. Your name. Words for food, water, hunger. Words for—um"—he hesitated—"calls of nature."

I nodded. He had not asked me to make friends with them, only to treat them as animals. To make them biddable.

"You will be my gillie—do you know what that means?" he asked.

I shook my head.

"In the highlands of Scotland, not far from where I myself was born, a gillie is a manservant who helps his laird—his master—with the wild game. You shall be my gillie—and the Lord's. And you shall help with these very particular wild creatures."

"Gillie," I said, reminding myself to write it down.

"First, though, we should decide on names for them. I thought Mary and Ann would do."

Marveling at my courage, I answered, "Sir, they already have names."

"What!" He took his glasses off at once and began rubbing them vigorously with his handkerchief.

I persisted in my not-quite lie. "Yes, sir. Their names are Amala and Kamala. The little one is Amala, the bigger one Kamala."

"Mohandas, Mohandas, what an incredible boy you are! Kamala, lotus. Amala, yellow flower. Not exactly appropriate, but one never knows." He smiled at me, a crooked little smile that touched his mouth briefly. "And so the miracle grows. They have told you their names. God's wonders never cease in this strange barbaric land. A lotus and a yellow flower. Have they spoken anything else?"

I shook my head and looked to the ground. Suddenly my lie loomed large before me. Should I confess it? I wondered. Would he guess?

"Do not worry, Mohandas," he said, taking my chin in his hand and slowly forcing my face up toward his. I stared into his bright blue eyes. "Do not worry. They will say more. One's name, it is thought, is the first thing learned and the last forgot. Names are powerful, my boy. That is why in the Bible God hides from Moses His own ineffable name."

The blue eyes were as wide as pools. I felt myself drowning in them. I blinked several times.

Mr. Welles patted my head. "My boy, my boy, these two babes of the wood shall be your special charge now. Since they have spoken only to you, they have—for whatever reason—singled you out. You must write in your English journal about them so that when they begin to tell their great and wonderful story, we shall have it all set down."

"I have already begun writing of them," I said, the words, as usual, difficult to say.

"Good boy," Mr. Welles answered. He turned from

me and sat down behind his desk, took out his pipe and began the long ritual of lighting it. "Will you let me see what you have written?"

"It is . . . it is in cipher," I said, all my shame welling up. I was certain he could see the lies.

"If I give you another book, will you translate it for me—the part about the wolf-girls only?" His brief smile stumbled across his mouth again.

I nodded, Indian style, somewhere between yes and no, and did not even attempt to smile back.

# THE GILLIE

### ◆◆◆

AMALA AND KAMALA. IT IS STRANGE HOW THOSE TWO TOOK
up my days. I was rarely with Rama and the other
children except at meals, and I did not miss them, although until the arrival of the wolf-girls they had been
my only companions. Instead I followed the wolf-
children around, followed as closely as I dared, watching
as they crawled or scuttled around the compound, in
the part of the courtyard shaded by the giant jackfruit
tree.

Their loincloths were continually soiled with dirt and
dog droppings and their own untended filth. As fast as
Mrs. Welles changed them, she was never fast enough,

and I was not allowed to do that office for them. Yet I found that their filth did not offend me. Amala and Kamala were like infants or baby animals, blissfully unaware that what they did might wrinkle the noses of fastidious human beings.

Indira openly mocked them. Rama made his abhorrence clear by the way he walked around them, never looking directly at them, not even letting his eyes slide toward the corner they had made their own. But the open hatred of Indira and Rama and the others did not trouble me. I simply did not care what they thought. Amala and Kamala had been put in *my* charge. I was Mr. Welles' gillie, eager for my duties.

After a while the wolf-girls became used to me. I was a part of their surroundings, and they accepted me as they accepted their dish of food or the lantana bushes or the gate that shut them away from the gardens.

By the second week of my gilliehood, the little one, Amala, came onto my lap. I was sitting quietly near them, and suddenly, without warning, she bounded playfully up to me and settled herself on my outstretched legs. She was very light. Carefully I patted her head, then her bare shoulder. Neither girl would yet accept the cotton shift without ripping it off, though they tolerated the loincloths, which were firmly sewed, rather than pinned or tied, into place.

Amala began to hum under her breath, a sound that was part purr and part tune. She shoved her face under my arm, sniffing and snuggling—the kind of thing I had seen her do with her sister, the most basic animal communication.

I ran my hand along her backbone. It was knobby and bumpy, full of ridges. There were scars, too, all along her back.

Suddenly she became wet and, without thinking, I shoved her off my lap. She lifted her face to mine, and though there was little expression there, she managed to look hurt and scurried back to the wall. But she was to come up to me and snuggle frequently after that. Wet or dry, she made no distinction, though I tried to teach her the difference.

Kamala, though, retained a certain aloofness, a kind of quiet dignity. She felt—I am sure of it—that she resided in that gulf between animal and human. She seemed puzzled by it, moving her head from side to side, considering. Often I would look at her as she rested, head on arm. Unlike Amala, who had moments of great playfulness mixed with long hours of sleep, Kamala was almost always alert, her eyes open and interested in everything. There were wrinkle lines on her forehead, as though she were thinking about how she was different from the dogs and different, as well, from me.

I helped her the only way I could. I would creep on

hands and knees to within a foot of her and sit silently for a long, still moment until she was no longer restive. I would say my name, say hers, in a clear but gentle voice, then pat the ground.

"Mohandas," I said, pointing to my chest.

"Kamala," I answered myself, pointing to her, adding in a fair imitation of Mr. Welles' voice, "Everything has a name." Then, patting the ground beside me, I would end, "Home. Home."

Her forehead would wrinkle again, and she would blink, but she did not speak.

It was a strange time for me. The wolf-girls and I were left alone by the other children. Except for meals, which I still took with the others, and high tea under the *ansh* tree, and brief chats with Rama at bedtime about insignificant things, I led a separate life. I wrote down what I saw and read it out loud to Mr. Welles each evening. If he was distressed at the slow progress the wolf-children made, he did not say, and he did not ask again about their ability to speak. He listened with a quiet concentration, smoking his pipe, his forehead as wrinkled as Kamala's, as I read, and only once or twice commented on my grammar or corrected my sentences in a perfunctory way.

The weeks of the dry season passed quickly, but the monsoon did not start until June fourth. Then we were all forced to stay indoors much of the time, listening to the battering rain shake the orphanage roof. Our gardens turned into jungles and every night it was hard to sleep because of the sweet, cloying scent of jasmine that covered us like an unwanted blanket. On the east side of the house the acres of mango and jackfruit and palm blossomed. The coleus and poinsettias overflowed their earthenware tubs. Only the section of English flowers, which Mr. Welles tended so carefully—violets and nasturtiums and phlox—suffered in the rain and heat, turning brown or growing in wild and irregular straggles of stem, leaf, and flower.

Amala and Kamala stayed out in the compound under a sheltering roof, but whenever the rains stopped, they would leave their little net-covered lean-to to lie outside, a rain cloud of mosquitoes buzzing over their heads.

Amala began to sleep more and more. She stopped eating, drank but little. After two days of it I spoke fearfully to Mrs. Welles.

"She does not wake up," I said.

"It is this rain," said Mrs. Welles, dabbing at her forehead with a handkerchief and sighing. Everything in the house seemed damp. "How the good Lord made a country with such weather is beyond me. I have always wondered that you Indians have prospered at all. Weeks of battering rains, months of stifling heat."

"She has not awakened at all today," I repeated.

Mrs. Welles looked down at me. "Not at all, Mohandas? Are you sure?"

"Not once," I said, only slightly exaggerating. Amala had looked up—once. Her eyes had been glazed over. I did not think she had recognized me.

Mrs. Welles hesitated no longer, but gave a running commentary on her own faults as she saw them as we strode along the corridor. "I should not have left their care so much to you, Mohandas, but there were the accounts to do. And the quarter-year report to help Mr. Welles with. Oh, you have done well, and you have been infinitely patient with the wolf-children. I would not have thought it possible of an adolescent boy. But you *are* a boy. And a native at that, for all you are intelligent and a Christian now. But I should have set aside the reports. Oh, Mohandas, she has not waked once?"

Amala *was* awake when we got to the wall. She was moaning and thrashing convulsively. Mrs. Welles picked her up and carried her into the house. Amala was so weak she did not seem to notice.

Kamala followed us to the doorway. The sound of her howling protest followed us down the hall.

Mrs. Welles brought Amala into the sickroom and laid her down in one of the cribs.

"Quick, fetch Mr. Welles," she said. Then, almost as an afterthought, she added, "And some ice from Cook."

She looked down at Amala and shook her head.

Suddenly I was afraid. I ran swiftly to Mr. Welles' study, practicing what I would say, and so great was my worry I entered without knocking. He looked up, surprised at my intrusion.

"Mohandas!"

"Your lady wife bids you come at once," I said. "To the sickroom. It is Amala."

"The younger one?" he asked, rising.

I nodded. "Ice," I managed, my voice breaking on that single word. Then I turned and ran down the hallway, turned right and then right again into the kitchen. Behind me, I knew, the other children were gathering. I could hear their bare feet pattering along the floor.

Cook was sitting in the rocking chair Mrs. Welles had given her as a peace offering, a gift to make her stay despite the burden of the wolf-children. Cook took many rockings during her day now, and meals were even scantier and less appetizing than before. She looked up as I ran in, but only the widening of her eyes showed she was disturbed.

"Mrs. Welles needs ice," I said.

She grunted and gestured with her hand toward the icehouse outside, signaling me to get it myself.

I went through the door. It was raining again, but I ran quickly to the little house that lay under the mounds of dirt insulation. Until I had come to The Home, I had never seen ice. Opening the door, I was engulfed in the cool air. I coughed, and my breath plumed out before me. I took the ice pick from its hook on the wall and managed to chip off several large pieces, which I wrapped with some linen cloth hanging by the door.

I raced back to the sickroom, trailed by most of the children.

Mr. Welles was there. And Rama. There was now a stick of incense burning in the holder by the door. From outside came the sound of Kamala's ceaseless howls and the patter of rain.

Taking the ice from me, Mrs. Welles spoke to the three of us, her former mood of self-condemnation gone. "Mohandas, you must go outside and do what you can to comfort that child. She knows something is wrong, though I doubt she understands. Rama, you must run into town and fetch Dr. Singh. Hurry! David, my dear, I will need your help. We must bathe her with ice to bring down the fever until the doctor gets here. She is burning up. And we must get liquids down her, too. Barley water will be best."

No one moved.

"Now!" said Mrs. Welles.

Rama leaped away, and I, with a backward glance at the huddled figure in the crib, pushed through the knot of children at the door.

"Is she dying?" asked Indira, her eyes glittering.

I did not answer her with words; my look was enough. She scattered the others with the same sounds and hand movements she used to chase the guinea fowl from their eggs. I ignored them and went outside.

When Kamala saw me coming, she scampered back to her hut and was quiet for a moment. Then, when she realized I did not have Amala with me, her howls began anew, and I felt, with a longing so intense it burned in my chest, that I wanted to howl along with her.

# KAMALA ALONE

◆◆◆

DR. SINGH CAME AND STAYED ALL NIGHT, AND MR. AND MRS.
Welles kept watch with him.

As the oldest boys, Rama and I were ordered to take
turns being the runners for whatever the doctor might
need, but Rama, after waiting up the first hours, woke
me and spoke urgently.

"I will help those evil creatures no longer," he said.
"She whimpers like a dog, and the other one howls."
His eyes looked haunted.

I stared at the floor as I answered him. "I will do it
all."

He had the good grace not to thank me.

And so it happened that I was the only child who kept the long vigil. Twice I was actually sent to fetch something—once for a fresh basin of water and once for more ice. The rest of the time I crouched, unnoticed, in the corner of the sickroom and watched while Dr. Singh bent over Amala, ministering to her. She lay knees to chin, sweat beading her body. Mrs. Welles bathed her frequently with the ice water, and Mr. Welles read psalms from the Bible and begged God not to let the little miracle die.

Occasionally Amala convulsed, her arms and hands and legs reaching out in shaking spasms. Then it took all three of them to hold her. At each convulsion, Kamala outside the sickroom window set up a tremendous howling, and I, too, shook in response.

Mr. Welles said sharply each time, "Go to her, Mohandas. Keep her quiet. Her howls are frightening this little one," although it was quite clear by then to all of us that Amala was long past caring or hearing.

I ran outside and sat as close to Kamala as I dared, crooning, "It will be all right, Kamala. It will be all right. Mohandas promises, everything will be all right."

But it was not all right. Amala died before dawn.

Dr. Singh's pronouncement was cold and clinical. "Worms," he said. "And dysentery, which has led to dehydration. Possibly nephritis as well. And goodness knows what else." He wiped his hands on a towel as he spoke, then rubbed sleep from his eyes. His pointed beard waggled as he talked.

The incense burning fitfully did little to disguise the smell of sickness and death or the sharp odor of disinfectant in the room.

The other children were up and crowding into the doorway. Indira and Veda cried noisily, and Preeti, head cocked to one side, sniffled. Krithi and the other little ones merely stared. Rama had no readable expression on his face. But Cook, who bullied her way into the room, looked slightly pleased, as if to say, "I told you so."

"And the other one?" Mr. Welles asked, gesturing outside with his head.

Kamala would not let the doctor near her until Rama held her legs and I her arms. Dr. Singh examined her teeth and her throat and listened to her chest.

"Remarkable," he said. "Remarkable," though he did not say why. He left sulfa powder for the worms.

"I would bury the child's body as soon as possible because of the danger of infection. And away from here," he said, looking pointedly at Kamala.

"Oh, yes, yes," Mrs. Welles said to him. "She digs up the dogs' buried bones, you know." Then, as if shocked at what she had just suggested, Mrs. Welles held her handkerchief to her mouth and sobbed.

"We will bury her in the churchyard," Mr. Welles assured him.

They left the house and walked Dr. Singh to the gate under the protection of umbrellas. It was like a small funeral procession, the nodding black canopies marking the pace.

I went back to the sickroom. Amala still lay on the crib mattress. Some part of me had been sure she was still alive, but she had not moved. She lay straight in her death as she had never lain in her life.

I heard footsteps behind me as I began to cry. Turning, I saw it was Mr. Welles.

"Perhaps," I said, stumbling over the words, "we should never have taken them from the jungle."

"Nonsense, Mohandas," he answered sternly, his voice slightly ragged with emotion, "they are humans, not animals, and therefore possess a soul. It is our duty to see that their souls glorify God."

I looked over at the pathetic corpse laid out in the crib. I saw no glory there.

Amala was buried by the carters at noon, and none of us was allowed to witness it.

Though Kamala's face was devoid of emotion, she spent the rest of the day ranging through the compound in obvious distress, sniffing places that her sister had frequented. When Mrs. Welles served her food, she only picked at it, though she drank the barley water, which Mrs. Welles had liberally laced with more of the worming medication. By evening she had stomach cramps and sat with her arms cupped around her belly, moaning. The next morning she passed a great mass of wormy stool with large red roundworms as thick as my little finger.

Mr. Welles rejoiced at that. He called us out to inspect it.

"Look, children, she is expelling her animal nature. Soon you will see a great change in her."

Exhausted by crying and by the continual pounding of the rains, I went to sleep that night much earlier than usual, but I was awakened around midnight by a strange, forlorn sound. It was not the sound of *dholes*, the wild dogs, on the hunt, though it had that same eerie quality. It was Kamala crying as she had done the first few nights after she had been brought to The Home. The sound went on and on and on.

I tried putting the pillow over my ears, but managed to muffle the noise only slightly. I wondered that she had not awakened the entire household. At last I got out of bed, climbed over the windowsill, and dropped into the compound.

The rain had stopped for a while, leaving an uncomfortable heavy mist and the profusion of flower smells. A thin, pale moon shone down.

As my feet touched the ground, the clock in Mr. Welles' study started chiming the hour.

Kamala lifted her head at my coming.

I stopped several feet away from her and squatted, waiting as usual for her to become used to me before venturing closer.

No sooner had I settled on my heels than she crawled toward me and laid her head on my knees, making a sound somewhere between a moan and a sigh.

Very slowly I reached out and patted her head.

She did not move away.

I let my hand rest on her head for a minute, counting the seconds under my breath. Then I moved my hand to her shoulder. Her skin trembled under my fingers.

She breathed loudly once more, then suddenly sat up and stared at me, not into my eyes but taking in my face and body with a long glance.

I did not dare move, but I could feel the tears once again welling up in my eyes as I thought of little Amala lying dead in the crib.

Kamala's face was in shadow, though I could see the blue glint of her night-shining eyes. The moon lit my face, and the tears must have glistened on my cheeks.

She reached up a hand to my face; one finger rested curiously on the tear. Then she put that finger in her mouth, tasting the salt.

"Mohandas." I whispered my ritual, touching my

84

chest. Then I reached out toward her, but before I could say her name, she put that same hand out again and touched me on the collarbone.

"Mmmmdah," she stammered. "Mmmmdah."

For a moment I was stunned. In the silence I could hear the sound of the cuckoo singing *piu-piu-pee-pee-piu*, and the *pick-buzz* of insects. Then I exploded, "Yes. *Yes!* Mohandas. Mo-han-das!"

"Mmmmdas," she said, poking me hard in the chest. Then she put her head back and howled, a mournful farewell.

# WALKING OUT

◆◆◆

THAT DAY AND ALL THE DAYS THAT FOLLOWED, KAMALA
grew and changed. At first she seemed to search for her
sister, pacing back and forth along a specific trail as if
casting for Amala's scent. But at last she gave up and
focused on me instead. No longer did she hunch beside
the wall, scuttling over to her food dish and then back
again. Instead, whenever I appeared, she would pad
alongside me, sniffing at my heels or trying to hold onto
my hand.

"You have become her brother, Mohandas," Mr.
Welles said with approval, rubbing his glasses with the
handkerchief and nodding. "It is time now for her to

take her next step up the species ladder. As Mr. Darwin has taught us, man has ascended from apes, not descended from angels. Let us help lift our little miracle higher. Otherwise why has God sent her here to us?"

I moved my head slightly and, as usual, he took it as yes and so went on speaking.

"Mrs. Welles will continue to give her daily massages with mustard oil to strengthen her legs, but you must encourage her to stand upright. For only in that posture can she fully praise the Lord."

I refrained from mentioning the many people who bowed to their god, as I had read in the books in Mr. Welles' own library. Instead I began to envision how I might get Kamala to stand. She could run faster than I on all fours, but it was a strange, low maneuver.

"Perhaps," I said, remembering the dogs prancing on their hind legs before animal trainers at the *hâts*, "with a bit of food above her . . ." And there I faltered, my imagination having gotten me so far and no further.

"Excellent, Mohandas," Mr. Welles said, patting me on the head. "Try it at once. Now."

In the kitchen I begged a few pieces of uncooked chicken— a wing and a piece of skin. Cook gave them to me reluctantly, guessing that they were for Kamala. But as I had Mr. Welles' permission, she did not dare deny them to me.

I went outside, and Kamala came galloping up to me, sniffing the air eagerly with her broad, flat nose. She pawed at my leg.

"Look, Kamala," I said. "See what Mohandas has brought you." I held the chicken wing out above her head.

She spoke her one word. "Mmmmdas." Then she tried to take the chicken from me.

I held it higher, dangling it just out of reach.

She tried desperate little lunges at it, and at each movement I placed the chicken higher still.

At last she put her hands on my legs, then my waist, and pulled herself up, standing very uncertainly and clinging to me.

I put my arm around her waist, steadying her, and placed the chicken wing to her mouth.

She snapped it up and fell away from me, back onto all fours, scurrying to the corner of the compound where she ate her meals.

When she finished the little piece of chicken, she was back, begging for more.

I showed her the bit of skin I had, holding it above her. This time there was no hesitation. Using me as an ape would a tree, she stood and grabbed for the meat.

I let her fall and kept the chicken.

"You must stand, Kamala," I said. "Try again. Come. Come to Mohandas."

But she returned to the corner to sulk.

I walked over to her, for the lesson had only begun.

"See the chicken, Kamala," I said. "You know you want it. Come. Come to me."

It took almost five minutes more before greed won over pride, but at last she came, crawling over, whimpering piteously, her head lowered. "Mmmmdas," she cried. "Mmmmdas."

I bit my lip and reminded myself to be stern. I held the chicken up.

One hand on my leg, she raised herself and stood, holding out her hand.

I put the chicken skin in her mouth, but before she could drop down again, I grabbed both her hands in mine and forced her to stand upright.

"Come," I said. "Walk, Kamala. Walk." Then I stepped backward, forcing her to come toward me.

She hopped awkwardly.

"Good, Kamala. Walk," I said again, taking another step backward.

Again she hopped.

Ten steps later I stopped, for it was obvious she was tired and cranky. I let her hands go, and she dropped down on all fours at once. I patted her on the head.

"Good Kamala," I said. "Good girl."

And so ended our first lesson in walking.

By the end of the monsoon season, in September, after many more such lessons, Kamala could walk upright, though never without food for encouragement and always with some pain, for her back was slightly bowed and so were her legs. But Mrs. Welles continued the mustard oil massages, which Kamala seemed to enjoy, and which seemed to ease the worst of the aches.

Once Kamala started walking on two legs regularly, Mrs. Welles insisted she had to wear a dress. And to tell the truth, I was glad of that, for as she ate more— vegetables and rice were added to her diet—she had grown healthier, and she began to fill out. No longer did her skin pull so tightly over her bones that one could discern the skeleton beneath. And too, with health came the early signs of her womanhood. It was an embarrassment to be with her if she went unclothed.

But she did not like her dress. The first time she was forced to wear it, she tried to tear it off again, pulling at the neck with frantic fingers, and growling.

"No!" I said sternly, slapping lightly at her hands.

She thought that a great game and pawed at me, the hated dress forgotten for the moment.

"Mohandas says *no!*" I repeated, holding her hands at her sides.

"Mmmmdas," she imitated, ending with a grunting sound. She did not struggle.

"Good girl," I said, though I did not let go of her hands to pat her on her head.

Just then Mr. and Mrs. Welles walked out into the compound.

"You are a miracle worker indeed, Mohandas," said Mr. Welles, smiling at me.

"Kamala listens to you, Mohandas," his wife added. "I cannot get her to say *my* name."

"Perhaps . . ." I began.

"No perhaps about it," said Mr. Welles. He turned to his wife. "I told you he is a fine lad. The brightest of the lot, even though he rarely speaks." Then, turning back to me, he finished, "*Words*, Mohandas. Words. See how the lack of words keeps her in her animal state? When she has attained the miracle of speech, which more than the opposable thumb separates man and beast, she will be free of her animal spirit entirely. Words will free you as well."

They stayed a minute more, contemplating Kamala, who fidgeted under their stares. Then they left, chatting about parish business. Mrs. Welles placed her hand on her husband's arm as they walked.

Kamala put her hand on the crook of my elbow. "Mmmmdas," she said, pulling me forward. She mumbled a succession of sounds, like a baby's babble, imitating Mrs. Welles.

I did not know whether to be disgusted or to laugh. In the end I did neither, but disengaged her hand from my arm and went indoors, where I knew she would not follow.

Later that same day Rama and I walked out of the schoolroom together. It had been months since we had spent time with each other, since before the trip to Godamuri. I realized suddenly how much I had missed him, and that was strange, for, in truth, I saw him every day. We studied together and slept in the same room. But since the arrival of the wolf-children, all between us had changed. I wondered if I had the proper words to tell him so, but I never got the chance to try.

"Mohandas," he said to me, his words tumbling over one another in Bengali, "Mr. Welles tells me that in a year I am to be apprenticed to a storekeeper in Midnapore. He sells cloth and woven goods and needs someone with a strong back and a head for figures. He will teach me how to tell good cloth from bad. I will live there as well, and I will have a trade. He is a Christian man, Mr. Welles says, and is doing this out of duty and love."

I wrinkled my nose, and Rama laughed, and it was so much like our old times together that I felt a great rush of affection for him.

"Indira says that I should be a soldier, not a shopkeeper, with a uniform of red and gold. But what does she know? I will be in the city and will be treated as a man there, not a boy or some Englishman's lackey. And I will have money for rice beer and sweets."

I clapped him on the back, for I knew that being on his own was his greatest wish. Then I looked at the ground as if the words I wanted were growing there at my feet.

"I will miss you, Rama."

He grabbed me by the shoulder. In English he said, "It is not for a year. And besides, you have your dirty little wolf-girl. You will not miss me." He laughed when he said it, but there was an edge to his voice.

"You . . . you have been *jealous!*" I said, amazed that I had never realized this before, never realized that I had been as much Rama's friend as he was mine.

"Of *that?*" He pointed through the door and out into the compound where Kamala waited for me.

For the first time I saw her as Rama did. Bent over, with legs and arms as gnarled and crippled and thin as those of an old, old woman, her eyes were focused on a lizard crawling up the wall. Her fingers twitched as she watched it. I remembered with burning shame how, in the past, she had occasionally pounced on lizards and eaten them alive. Her skin was still like parchment stretched over bone, and the deep hollows of her cheeks matched the hollows of her eyes. How could Rama have been jealous of my attentions to such a creature?

Kamala turned and saw me then and gave her inhuman smile, just lips pulled away from sharp yellow teeth. There was no mirth or humor in that grimace. It was a dog's baring of fangs.

"Mmmmdas," she cried out, holding up her arms.

I wondered that I had ever thought such a mumble was really my name.

I turned from her and said, "Rama, I am sorry . . ." but he was already gone.

Mr. Welles came out of his study. "Ah, there you are, Mohandas. I thought that today you could take Kamala out for a walk on the *maidan* for the first time. She trusts you enough so that I doubt she will run away."

I nodded sullenly. I wanted nothing more to do with her.

"Be sure to fill your pockets with some sweets," he added. "You know how she has developed a taste for such things. And take her on a leash."

Because I had been ordered to do so, I went to Cook and got a few of the biscuits she had made for afternoon tea. She was not pleased that they were for the wolf-girl.

94

All the while, Kamala waited for me at the door. I made a face when I saw her there, for I was seeing her now through Rama's eyes: a pathetic parody of a girl.

"Come on," I said, gesturing with my hand. She came readily. I put a dog collar around her neck and attached a leash. She did not seem to mind.

Then I opened the great wooden gate, lifting the latch and pushing hard with my shoulder. Kamala paid no attention to the process but capered around my feet on all fours, grunting and panting and making animal noises.

When I finally pushed open the door and she could see outside for the first time, she hung back.

"Come on," I shouted at her, and started out, tugging on the leash.

Reluctantly she followed, standing upright and taking timid half-steps.

Open and flat, the *maidan* had once been used to drill soldiers when The Home had been headquarters for the Second Rajputs, an Indian regiment. There were now bushes growing up along the parade route, and a few spindly trees. It was a good place to play ball.

When Kamala realized how wide open the *maidan* was, she refused to move farther and stood there, trembling. She grabbed onto my arm and nearly pulled me over. I had to remove her hand from my elbow forcibly. Then I looked into her eyes, those frightened, shifting animal eyes.

"Kamala, come," I said. "We are going to walk around the *maidan*. The *sahib* Welles has ordered it so."

At Mr. Welles' name, she looked over her shoulder back at the orphanage. I pulled on her hand and the leash simultaneously and began to drag her with me. "Kamala, come."

The *maidan* was dry, and our feet raised soft little puffs of dust. Kamala twisted around to look at the prints we left behind.

I pulled her forward.

About halfway across the *maidan* we came upon the carcass of a cow. Vultures were already at it, tearing greedily at its rotting flesh. Kamala stopped and sniffed the air, turning toward the dead beast. She licked her lips, started to pull at her leash.

"Kamala, no," I said sharply, giving the line a quick tug.

She broke suddenly from my grasp, tearing the leash from my hand and ran—not toward the cow, as I feared, but back to the open gate—crablike and scrambling on all fours.

I ran after her as fast as I could, but I could not catch up.

She stopped at the gate and pulled herself erect, using the wall. She was scarcely out of breath, but by the time I reached her, I was breathing heavily, and my stomach heaved.

"Kamala," I panted, raising my hand, prepared to scold.

She smiled that strange animal smile at me and put her hand out, touching my chest.

"Mmmmdas," she said. She pointed to her own chest. "Kmmmmala." Then she pointed in toward the compound. "Home," she said, as clearly as if she had spoken the word every day of her life. "Home."

# WORDS

◆◆◆

OH, THE RIVER FLOW OF WORDS THAT FOLLOWED AMAZED us all. She was never easy to understand, but slowly we all learned Kamala's peculiar way of speaking. She would concentrate her effort in her face, muscles straining, forehead wrinkled, pushing out a single word at a time, often foreshortened by a syllable or two. She never learned true sentences, and curiously enough, she never learned to say the words yes and no. Just a narrowing of her big eyes indicated no; a wide-open grin meant yes. Everything she said was in the present tense, as if the past did not exist for her.

After my name, her name, and "home," she quickly

learned these words: milk, rice, meat, flower, tree, dog, bird, glass, hand, egg, cow, goat, cat, water, bath, mirror, dress, dirty, ball, horse, cart, garden, in, out, shoe, doll, give.

"*And whatsoever Adam called every living creature,*" intoned Mr. Welles in his Bible-quoting voice, "*that was the name thereof.*" He puffed a cloud of pipe smoke into the air.

"I hesitate to see where a shoe or a ball or a cart is a living creature, Mr. Welles," Mrs. Welles said, laughing. Indeed, we were all laughing as Kamala went around the courtyard touching things and naming them back to us.

She was like a large baby, and we rewarded her efforts as we would those of a small child, clapping and encouraging her further. She responded by going faster and faster.

For an afternoon she was a wonder, and we played the naming game with her. Even Cook joined in, our laughter bringing her away from her rocker. She came out with a plucked chicken in her hands and pointed to it, saying, "Meat, meat."

Kamala answered by trying to grab the uncooked fowl from Cook's hand, and Cook ran back to the kitchen screaming, and that was the end of her participation.

After an hour of the game Mr. Welles put his hands up for us to stop. "Let us hold a Thank Offering Service right here, right in the courtyard under the eye of God."

Indira whispered to Rama, and I overheard, "I thought God could see us wherever we were."

Rama nudged her in the ribs, and they both giggled.

But we knelt down because Mr. Welles requested it, untroubled by Indira's whispered blasphemy or by the heavy smell of the charcoal and cow dung smoke from the lunchtime fires signaling Cook's assault on the chicken. We knelt and gave thanks for Kamala's liberation by words.

Kamala knelt, too, and hummed tonelessly throughout the entire litany.

The afternoon passed, and though Kamala learned several dozen new words, the wonder of it was over. It was just as when the monsoon rains pass and it is difficult to remember in the heat of the dry season how much we hated all that rain.

Now that Kamala had words enough, she needed me less. Anyone could understand her and make her obey, and so I returned to my regular studies and my regular chores, both relieved and saddened. My notebook began to refer to people other than the wolf-girl.

She became a part of the activities of The Home, exploring inside The Home as well as out, though there were some places off limits to her—the kitchen, the English garden, and beyond the wall. She became fas-

cinated especially with certain of the children's games—
the boys' spinning tops, the girls' rag dolls. And while
no one would let her play with their toys, she was allowed to sit quietly and watch. Often she would mumble under her breath as they played, "Give. Give." But
no one gave anything to her.

Finally Mrs. Welles noticed and made her a dolly of
her own, from a piece of bright red material, for red
had become her favorite color.

The day Kamala was given her dolly, Indira turned
sulky, for until that time she had had the brightest,
newest-looking doll. She never played with it, which
was why it was so clean. And though she should have
been too old to care about Kamala's doll, she made her
displeasure known. Loudly.

"*She* should have been given a dog-brown doll," Indira said. "A doll with a tail."

Preeti giggled, one slim hand held over her mouth.

"And pups at its teats," added Indira daringly.

Both Veda and Preeti laughed. Encouraged, Indira
continued, "Krithi, bring that dog's doll to me."

Krithi shook his head miserably.

Indira stamped her foot and looked around. She saw
me in the doorway but did not dare ask me. Still she
did not want to stop the game; to do so would have
shamed her before her followers.

No one volunteered.

"You are *all* dogs!" Indira shouted, frowning menacingly. "I will get it myself."

She went over to the corner where Kamala sat, rocking and petting the doll.

"Come here, Kamala. Come to Indira. Come," she sang out in a cozzening voice. Anyone else hearing her use that tone would have been immediately on guard, for it promised danger. But not Kamala. She stood up at once and went over to Indira eagerly.

Indira's hand, as quick as a cobra, reached out and snatched the red doll.

Kamala howled, crying out in her peculiar voice, "Give. Give. Doll. Give." But Indira paid no attention.

Then Kamala tried to grab the doll back. Indira flung it quickly to Krithi, who caught it with a look of surprise on his face.

Kamala scrambled over to Krithi, growling, and he tossed the doll to Veda.

She caught the doll by a leg and threw it at once to Preeti. But Preeti, with her weak eyes, did not see the doll coming, and it dropped in front of her. Kamala pounced upon the doll, clutching it to her chest and grunting, "Doll. Doll. Doll." She bared her teeth and looked so fierce that the game stopped at once.

The others ran across the compound and through the little gate to Mr. Welles' garden, where Kamala had been forbidden to follow.

I had not moved or spoken the whole time, and when she passed me, Kamala gave me a look compounded of disgust and despair. Shamed, I turned away, bumping into Rama, who had just come into the hall.

"Mohandas, what is it?" he asked.

"A game," I mumbled, and left.

After that day Kamala took the doll with her everywhere, dragging it along when she crawled, sleeping with it, holding it while she ate, until it was scarcely more that a tattered piece of red material. She did not seem to know or care whether it was a doll or a rag, just that it was hers and in her hand.

Indira, of course, was ecstatic, and in her happiness left Kamala alone. She took her own doll out, displaying it with pride.

"See," she said, "see how beautiful *my* doll is."

The other children admired it on cue.

Rama, when he heard her, only laughed. "Girls!" he said. "How silly."

But I dared to look directly at Indira, speaking so only she and I could hear. "It is just rags," I said. "Just rags."

She hit me with the doll and went inside.

Kamala was more careful around Indira after that, but she was still fascinated by the children and followed them, always a beat behind. She even took her turn hauling on the rope that pulled the *punkah* that kept Mr.

Welles' study cool. In fact, she loved to do that so much that we all let her take our turns, for it was, in truth, a dull and boring chore.

Anyone seeing her or hearing her push out the few words she could manage would have known her for a moon child, slow in the mind.

Even Mr. Welles ignored her, forgetting the miracle he had prayed for, or at least changing his mind about its character. It was clear to everyone, and especially to me, that she would never tell us stories about her life with the wolves. Indeed three words together were the most she ever managed, though it was also clear that she could understand considerably more than she could express.

But as Mr. Welles ignored her and I left her alone, more and more often Rama began to seek her out. It almost appeared that he was paying her court for, in the season of the winter sun, with the help of Cook's nourishing—if unappetizing—meals, she began to blossom into a real woman. Her mind might not have developed much, but her body did. Her silences, so different from Indira's ceaseless sarcasm and Veda's whispered confidences, appealed to Rama. And she was so biddable. If he wanted her to fetch something for him, all he had to do was ask and she scampered off to get it. He no longer saw her as evil but as saved, and he was fascinated by her pliant nature, her eagerness to please.

Once I found him sitting with her just outside the gate, on the edge of the *maidan*. She was catching lizards. Her fingers, like quick brown vines, flashed out and trapped one of the little reptiles as it climbed the wall, then as suddenly set it free.

"Look, look," he said to me. "See how quick she is."

"See, see how slow you are," I retorted. "I am halfway through our chores, yours and mine."

He did not apologize but got to his feet. Kamala followed and, to my chagrin, took his hand, walking sedately by his side.

"Ram, Kmmmmla in," she said.

I was secretly pleased to see that when she walked she still held her shoulders hunched over. No sooner had that thought formed than I was ashamed of it. Rama did not seem to notice the succession of emotions crossing my face, and for that I was thankful.

Another time I heard him leave at night, out the window. I thought he was off to Tantigoria again after weeks of remaining at home. I resolved to wait up and speak with him when he returned. But when I heard whispering from outside, I knew he had gone only as far as Kamala's hut. And though I could not make out what he was saying, I could clearly hear her peculiar laughter, echoing, "Hoo—hooo—hoo." Since she did not understand word jokes, I knew he had to be tickling her, and when I heard him laughing back, I did not know whom I hated most—Rama or Kamala or myself.

I was not the only one who noticed Rama's interest or guessed at the reasons for it. Although she made no mention of it, Indira knew, and her anger began to grow.

I reveled in it. If I could not do something about my own private shame, I knew Indira would.

At first she showed her anger in subtle ways. She took to pulling the flowers from Veda's hair. When Veda complained, Indira pinched her above the elbow. Veda carried many little black-and-blue pinch marks, a tattoo of bruises, on both her arms for days.

Then Indira began to imitate Krithi unmercifully, walking beside him and limping. When he asked her to stop, she walked away from him, exaggerating the limp even more and sticking her thumb in her mouth so there was no doubt who was the butt of her mimicry. When Krithi turned to me for help, I looked away.

The little ones were soon in terror of her attacks, and not a one would be in a room alone with her. They ran out screaming the moment she entered.

And then she stole my notebook. I did not see her do it, but it could not have been anyone else.

Why did I say nothing? I think my shame and anger and pain were too great, and I believed I deserved to be weak and unhappy. For a week we all bore the brunt of Indira's dark anger, all except Rama and Kamala. Indira never once menaced them, though it was they, not the rest of us, who were the cause of her ire.

Mrs. Welles took Indira aside and spoke strongly to her. Krithi told me of it, for he had listened at the door. "I could not hear all the words, Mohandas," he said. "But Mrs. Welles was loud and angry. Buzz-buzz-buzz like a mosquito." He popped his finger back into his mouth, a cork in a bottle.

"It is not Indira's fault," I said. "She is unhappy."

"*She* is impossible," whispered Veda. "*I* am unhappy." It was then she uncovered her arms and I saw the pattern of bruises that Indira's fingers had imprinted on her flesh.

Did I resolve then to champion the other children? I did, but I need not have worried. After Mrs. Welles' lecture, Indira kept to herself, nursing her unhappiness, letting it grow. She was still sickly sweet to Rama, and I knew she would turn her abilities for mischief toward Kamala. I tried to guess what she might do. As it turned out, my guesses were too feeble, my change of heart too late. Indira had a positive genius for torture, and in Kamala she had discovered a victim who could not easily tattle.

# INDIRA'S WAR

◆◆◆

WE KNEW INDIRA WAS A BULLY AND A SNEAK, BUT NO ONE
was ever to know the full extent of her anger. Even
after, for Kamala never had enough words to tell—only
grimaces and tears—we could only imagine what she
had been through. But what I did not know I recon-
structed, and what I did not see I guessed.

Indira organized the other children against Kamala,
and to be free of Indira's torments themselves, they
gladly followed her lead. Only Rama and I were left
out.

Indira urged Krithi to put curry powder on Kamala's
meat though we all knew she ate her meat without spices,

even without salt. Indira supplied Veda and Preeti with soap shavings for Kamala's drinking water. She gave the little ones sticks, promising them candies, which her parents sent her each month from Calcutta, if they would shake the sticks in Kamala's face whenever they could. I know all this to be true, for the others confessed it later. But these were only skirmishes in Indira's war.

The real battle lines were drawn between Indira and Kamala. And only Indira knew the reasons why.

It was a week after Rama began paying attention to Kamala that the bruises started showing, little strings of them like beads, along the insides of Kamala's arms. When questioned, she shook her head and hummed a wordless little tune, like a mantra, sworn to a strange kind of secrecy by her tormentor. The only thing she said, when Mrs. Welles questioned her about the bruises, was, "Bhoo, bhoo, bhoo," which meant nothing to us.

Then one morning she had two enormous bruises on each ankle, and the next day a black eye.

Mrs. Welles discussed it with her husband in his study, and I, crouched down behind the desk, looking over books on the lowest bookshelf, listened.

"I don't like it, David," she said, her hands clasped together.

"Children do get bruises, my dear," he answered. "Look at Krithi—he is constantly black-and-blue. And didn't Veda recently have an armful of bruises? And

Preeti spent much of last rainy season immobilized from a fall? These things happen. Kamala is a tough little thing, though. She has had to be. I expect she is just going through a stage."

"David, I have questioned the children thoroughly on this, and they profess to be as puzzled as I. And Kamala only hoots mournfully when I ask her. But these bruises— new ones appear every day. I am worried that she may have some disease, some illness that manifests itself in bruising first. I am going to send for Dr. Singh."

Mr. Welles stood up, almost tripping over me, but otherwise ignoring my presence. Opening the door, he ushered Mrs. Welles out. "Very well, my dear, the health of the children is your concern, as their minds and souls are mine. Do what you think best. I must get back to my report for the *Diocesan Record*. I am mentioning the wolf-children in the hope that interest in their story and conversion will stimulate an interest in our work here at The Home and secure us better funding for the coming year."

He closed the door after her and returned to his desk, busying himself with the papers there. Quite soon I heard the scratching of his pen across the page. Holding the copy of *A Thousand and One Nights*, which Mrs. Welles had read to us and which I had chosen to read for myself, I stood up quietly, prepared to go out.

"Mohandas," Mr. Welles said, never looking up

from the paper on which he was writing.

"Yes, sir."

"Do you know anything about these bruises?"

"No, sir."

"If you learn anything, will you tell me at once?"

"Yes, sir."

"Very well. Now you may go."

I reached the door.

"Mohandas." His voice stopped me.

I turned. He was looking at me, and when our eyes met, he put down his pen, took off his glasses, and reached into his pocket for the handkerchief.

"Has she spoken to you about her life with the wolves at all?" He began cleaning his glasses.

"She can say words like *cat* and *ball* and *dress* and . . ." I began as a way of explanation.

He sighed and put the glasses back on. "And . . ."

"I think she has forgotten her days in the jungle, sir," I ventured. "And she has no word for what is past."

His hands folded together on the desk in front of him. He suddenly looked quite old. "There are those who say that without words there is no memory, Mohandas."

"She has words now," I said.

"*Cat* and *ball* and *dress?*" he asked.

I nodded.

111

"Not words for what she knew in the jungle, though," he said.

"And no word for yesterday either, sir."

Mr. Welles picked up his pen once again. "Tell me if you find out anything more about the bruises," he said. "We will not bother Mrs. Welles about how or where you get that information." The pen started across the page again. It was a dismissal.

Although I had not stayed up at night for several weeks, I determined that this night I would. Rama's stuttering snore was my signal. I got out of bed, slipped on my trousers, but left my *kharom* behind. Wooden slippers make too much noise.

I climbed over the windowsill and dropped silently to the ground, practice having perfected the movement. There was only a sliver of moon.

I told myself that I was acting on Mr. Welles' direct orders, but in my deepest heart I knew it was more than that. I had acted foully, worse than a beast. Kamala had no one to protect her but me. I had to go and reclaim the heart of my dearest friend. The others had tried to make of her something she was not—a miracle, an enemy, a woman. I wanted her for what she was—my other self, different, full of unspoken words, and alone.

As I neared the corner where she slept at night, I heard whispering. I stopped.

112

It was Indira's voice. The words became clearer as I crept forward.

"You are an evil *bhut*. You are wicked. You are an animal. You deserve to be punished. Eater of carrion, drinker of blood. Eater of carrion, drinker of blood. Say it. Say, 'I am a *bhut*.' "

And the answering soft cry came, "Bhoo, bhoo, bhoo."

I ran ahead with a scream. I do not remember what words I used, but they flowed out of me like great rivers of fire. I slapped Indira and screamed and screamed until the lanterns were lit throughout the house and Mr. Welles and his wife and Cook and the children and the carters all came running.

They found Indira with blood running down from her nose, and a swollen eye, and me at the gate looking out at the shadowy *maidan*, where a scuttling figure ran on all fours past the stunted trees, past the rice fields, stopping only once to look back at the walled house behind her and giving a single long, drawn-out howl before disappearing into the dark recesses of the sal.

# THE SEARCH

◆◆◆

"KAMALA!" I CRIED INTO THE NIGHT, MY VOICE AN ANI-mal's howl of despair, but she did not stop again, and she did not answer.

Mr. Welles' deep boom of a voice called out after mine, and the children, like piping echoes, screamed her name as well.

Rama ran a few steps out onto the *maidan*; then he turned and looked hopelessly at us all crowded into the gate. "She is gone," he said.

At that, Mrs. Welles thrust a kerosene lantern into my hand. "Mohandas, Rama, you will accompany Mr.

Welles onto the parade grounds and search the outskirts of the jungle. She will not have gone far in."

"You are right, my dear. The lights will call her out. She is just frightened. I cannot think how this could have happened."

"Indira made it happen," I said angrily.

"Mohandas made it happen," Indira retorted, wiping her still-bleeding nose on her hand.

"Never mind," Mrs. Welles said, skillfully shepherding Indira toward the house. "Veda, bring me the carbolic and a towel. Preeti, you take charge of getting the other girls to bed. Krithi, you are to do the same with the boys. Come, children. Do not let this upset you. It is long past the time you should be asleep."

They were reluctant to leave the excitement but finally followed her inside. Only Cook and the two carters stayed by the gate.

And so Rama and I, trailing Mr. Welles, went across the *maidan* toward the great looming sal jungle. We carried lanterns, but Mr. Welles bore a more primitive rag and bamboo torch that gave even more light.

My feet found every stone and stick on the ground. I tried to ignore the hurt, thinking instead of how Kamala must have felt, fleeing alone into the dark, bewildered and betrayed.

We held the lanterns up high and called out her name every few steps. Mr. Welles swore once, quietly, under his breath, when he stumbled, and I realized that he, too, was barefoot.

Along one edge of the jungle, near the place where Kamala had entered, was a little stream. Never very full, even during the monsoon, it was now a trickle. I knew the green-and-brown scaled mahseer lay on the pebbly bottom. Pushing through the tall reeds, I held my lantern high. Along the far side of the stream, down a little way from where I stood, I could see hand- and footprints.

"Here," I called out.

Mr. Welles and Rama came at once.

"Very good, Mohandas. She crossed here all right." He held the torch high. It barely cleared the tops of the reeds.

"Kamalaaaaaa," he called out. "Come home. Nothing will hurt you anymore."

It was very quiet in the aftermath of his calling. The quiet seemed to deepen the dark. Our lights extended only a few feet into the sal, although we could see the stream and its bank and all the way to the bottom, where the shadowy mahseer stroked their fins back and forth. But the jungle itself was pitch-black and still.

"We cannot track her into the jungle at night," Mr. Welles said sensibly. "Not with only three of us. We must return to The Home. It will soon be light, and then we will go out again. The carters will help, and we can get extra men from Tantigoria." He lowered the torch. "Of course she will no doubt have come home on her own by then, poor frightened child." He did not mention the wild animals that roamed the sal, even this close to the city. He did not have to.

Rama suddenly spoke. In careful English he said, "She will *not* come home. She is a wolf now. She has returned to her ancestors."

"Nonsense, her ancestors were human, just as yours were. She was never a wolf. Just a deserted child, probably turned out by her village for being slow. These heathens are a primitive people and are still given to such inhuman displays," Mr. Welles said.

He waded back across the shallow pool.

"She is a wolf again," Rama whispered to me fiercely in Bengali.

I did not answer, for indeed I did not know which was the truth.

"Kamalaaaaaa!" It was Mr. Welles calling again. He lifted the torch up high, as if that helped him to listen, but he was greeted only by the silence that pervades the jungle right after a loud noise.

"Come," he called to Rama and me. "We will do no good standing here. We will wait at home, leaving the gate open and a lantern shining there as a beacon. You boys can take turns sleeping outside, and I will send one of the carters to the village so that all will be ready for

*117*

morning. But do not worry. She will surely come home."

What could I say? That light would not be an invitation to her now? That she could see in the sal at night as well as we could during the day? That I feared that she would, indeed, seek out her home—the white ant mound from which we had stolen her so many months before? But Mr. Welles would have had none of that thinking, and I did not have the words to convince him. So I followed him back without saying anything at all.

As soon as the carter had gone off down the road toward Tantigoria, I turned to Rama.

"I will watch first."

Rama agreed at once and went back to our room to sleep. I gave the household another fifteen minutes to settle down, and then, taking the lantern with me, I ventured back across the *maidan*, watching this time where I put my feet. I felt no regrets at my deception. I knew that only I could possibly find Kamala now.

I plunged through the reeds, then located the prints that she had left in the bank.

"Kamala?" I asked loudly, part plea and part calling. I expected no answer and got none.

Taking a deep breath, I waded through the shallow stream, feeling the tails of the mahseer touch me briefly as they sought to escape my intrusion. Then I clambered up the other side.

I did not have time to be paralyzed by fear. I did not have time to think. I had to look for Kamala, and I hoped that it would be time enough.

The sliver of moon that had helped light my way across the *maidan* was obscured by the sal canopy. I had only my lantern for light.

Something flew past my head, and by the smell I knew it was a fruit bat, though its leathery wings made no sound at all. It startled me and I nearly dropped the lantern, but I forced myself to be calm. I had no wolfish night sight, and without my light I would be helpless until dawn.

I pushed through the reeds and found myself in a tiny garden-size clearing. The heavy packed dirt gave no evidence of footprints, but making my way around the edge of the clearing, I found a place where the undergrowth had been badly disturbed. It was a trail of sorts, and trusting that the bushes had been broken by Kamala's passage and not by some larger animal, I plunged directly in.

Here the sal trees really began in earnest, and in the lantern light their pale trunks, mottled with lichens, gave back a quiet luminescence.

I walked for a long time and heard nothing, my ears unable to sort out from the silence the jungle noises and the beating of my own heart. But finally I stopped, and the jungle life that had ceased movement at my crashing passage resumed.

A light wind rustled the treetops, like the sound of pages being turned. I looked up, lifting the lantern as I did so. A loud *khouk khouk khouk* broke from the tree-tops as a langur signaled danger. The cry was taken up by the rest of the troop, and there was a sudden flurry of activity high above me.

I waited, and slowly the agitation in the sal canopy died down. At last a jungle fowl's harsh voice announced to the others that all was well.

I was suddenly aware that it was cold in the forest and that I had nothing but my trousers for warmth. Only if I kept moving, kept searching for Kamala, would I stay warm.

Looking around, I caused the lantern to bob and throw shadows that danced uncannily in and out of the trees. On one low bramble I noticed something that was at odds with the rest of the undergrowth. When I went over to it, I saw it was a piece of cloth, a colored print torn from a girl's dress. I did not remember what Kamala had been wearing, seeing in my mind's eye only the scuttling shadow fleeing across the *maidan*. But who else would have been deep in the jungle, running fast enough to tear her dress and leave a piece behind? I was on the right trail, and holding the piece of cloth to my cheek, I sighed—a foreign sound in the sal.

120

Near the thorns the trail of broken branches continued, and, farther in, I found another piece of cloth. I plunged into the thick creepers, not caring that I might disturb snakes or stinging insects, that I might fall into the pathway of a boar or a bear. All at once I felt myself a predator, as powerful as any, on the trail of my prey, and what were bear, snake, tiger, or boar to me?

A sudden break overhead in the creepers that laced the sal let in the sliver of moon, and an entire patch of forest was illuminated before me. Ahead I could see another clearing, much larger than the last, as large as the *maidan*. I made my way forward and stopped at the clearing's edge, looking for further clues.

Stones and trees were outlined by both moon and lantern, a sharper definition than I could have seen by day. I saw shadows of deer, surprised by my sudden appearance, disappear between the trees and a thick brake of bamboo.

"Chital," I said aloud. *"Axis axis."*

Something slithered away from my feet with a rasping sound, like sand over wood, and went back into the bushes.

And then, on the far edge of the clearing, I saw what I had, without realizing, been seeking: a tall white ant mound rising in tiers, outlined by the moon against the darker forest behind. Near it towered a giant tamarind tree.

I caught my breath. There. Kamala was there. With the wolves.

Then I shook my head. It was not, after all, Kamala's old home. We had destroyed that den ten months before, along with the wolves in it. And for me to have gotten to that clearing near Godamuri would have taken at least two nights and three days of travel, not a few midnight hours of stumbling through the sal. This was the *real* world, after all, not the world of Araby, and I was a *real* boy named Mohandas Jinnah, not a boy named Aladdin in a magic tale.

But it was too much of a coincidence that the footprints and the trail of broken branches and the pieces of material should have led me here, to an ant mound so like Kamala's early home, if she was not also somewhere around. And what better place to hide in than that tiered monument carved out by the ants? So, cautiously, I made my way across the clearing.

The ant mound was larger by half than the one from which Kamala had been torn. In the moonlight the beveled surfaces seemed stonelike, solid, new. But on closer inspection it was obvious that the mound had been abandoned long ago by its termite tenants. The domed roof was worn by wind and rain, and there was a large hole halfway up the side.

When I got right up to the mound, I circled it warily, hoping to find some sign of Kamala. On the far side, by a large entry hole, I found pieces of her dress, a section of the skirt that she had evidently flung off before going in, and the tattered red rag that had been her doll.

I knelt down and called into the hole, "Kamalaaaaa! It is I, Mohandas."

There was no answer.

"Please, Kamala, come out. Come home."

My own voice echoed around the clearing. Sighing heavily, I realized how cold I was. In the sal after midnight there is a sudden drop in temperature. In the winter months it can be fatal. The only shelter was before me. Shivering with the cold—and with fear—and pushing the lantern ahead of me, I crawled into the dark hole. I hoped that it was not the home of more than a lonely, frightened girl.

# IN THE WHITE ANT MOUND

◆◆◆

I FOLLOWED THE TWISTING TUNNEL. IT WAS SO NARROW MY
shoulders scraped the walls and I could not turn my
head to look behind. The light from the lantern illuminated only a few inches ahead before the tunnel took
another turn. I could scarcely breathe.

Although I could not have been crawling longer than
a few minutes, it felt like hours. My knees and one hand
and both shoulders were already scraped and raw. I
sweated and felt faint. Then I coughed, and the lantern
began to flicker. I swallowed another cough, but still
the lantern faded, having little air to feed its flame and
hardly any kerosene left at all.

*124*

Another turn and the lantern suddenly flared up. I realized, with a start, that I was passing the hole on the side of the mound. As my head came even with it, I peered outside. I could see, as through the wrong end of a telescope, a cluster of pale stars.

Then the tunnel turned once more, and as I followed it, the stars were gone.

Ahead the tunnel suddenly widened into a small cave. The light from the lantern shone on a dark form. It was Kamala, her knees clutched to her chest, unmoving.

I left the lantern and crawled to her.

"Kamala," I breathed into the silence. "It is Mohandas. Speak to me."

There was no indication that she heard, even that she still breathed.

I reached her side and put my palm on her back. The skin was cool and dry, but it rippled under my fingers as an animal's does when it is touched. At least she was alive.

"Kamala," I said, "do not be afraid. No one will hurt you. I am here. Your brother. Your friend. Mohandas is here."

She began to whimper, then to grunt and grind her teeth. She hugged her knees even more tightly.

I lay down behind her and put my arms on her shoulders. "Hush," I said. "Mohandas is here." I held her and soothed her with a whispered litany until we both fell into an exhausted sleep.

In the total dark there is no way of knowing how much time has passed. Awake and asleep become much the same. We woke, we slept many times in that den until the lantern burned out and I could distinguish things only by touch.

It might have been days, but it turned out to have been only hours when hunger growled in my stomach and woke me. Cramped from lying huddled around Kamala on the packed sand floor, I tried to stretch. My feet hit one part of the wall, my hand another. It was close in the den, difficult to breathe. I had to fight to remember who and what I was.

"Kamala, come. We cannot stay in here," I mumbled sleepily.

She whimpered again.

I knew then that she could not or would not help herself. If I wanted her to come out, I would have to drag her.

Feeling around, I finally found the lantern near the tunnel entrance and then the entrance itself. I stretched out until I could touch Kamala's heels, and I tried to pull her toward me, but she would not let go of her knees, and I could get no leverage with which to pull her.

"Please, Kamala," I begged. "Help me. We cannot stay here, or we will die."

The words meant nothing to her.

What could I do? I had no way to pull her resisting body to the tunnel entrance, and even if I could get her that far, I could not force her bent limbs to straighten and in that way pull her along the winding path. So I crept on my bruised hands and knees, passing the brilliant window of day, until I came out into the lighted forest.

It was already morning, and the clearing had a slight mist rising from a *nullah* that still had water in it. I slid down the steep embankment and splashed water on my face, then stuck my head into it and drank deeply.

Rubbing the drops from my eyes, I looked around. Lying against one bank of the *nullah* was a large stick, no doubt washed downstream by the recent rains. I picked up the stick and hefted it, then slammed it against the bank. It did not break.

Climbing back up, I mulled over my plan. I did not dare go back to The Home for help. What if Kamala died in the meantime? What if I could not find this clearing again? No, there was only one way.

I went back over to the mound and with the stick began to dig feverishly, stopping only once in a while to catch my breath.

I heard again, as if in a dream, Mr. Welles' voice in

the clearing near Godamuri, saying, "Dig!"

The packed earth was as hard as stone, and bits of the stick kept breaking off, but still I dug, widening the tunnel entrance, and then, when I remembered it, battering at the hole through which I had seen the stars.

After an hour's frantic shoveling I had torn away only one small section of the mound, but I would not stop, not even to go back to the *nullah* for another drink of water.

Every once in a while I called out Kamala's name. Not that I expected an answer, but I wanted to remind myself that she was still there. Tears coursed down my cheeks, making muddy tracks. Sweat poured off my back. My hands and knees and shoulders ached. I did not care. I dug.

Suddenly one section of the mound collapsed. I dropped the stick and began to root around in the dirt with my torn hands, throwing the dirt behind me and screaming Kamala's name.

I heard my own name in answer. Then strong arms were around me, and I looked up. Mr. Welles and Rama and the carters and several men I had never seen before were by my side.

"Mohandas, Mohandas, we have been so worried about you. And then we heard your screams. What are you doing?" Mr. Welles asked.

"It is Kamala. She is in the den," I said.

"Are you sure?"

I nodded.

"Dig!" Mr. Welles said to the men.

They had only hands and feet, too, for they had been carrying guns, not shovels. But they dug with a fury that matched mine, and they were big men—and strong.

Within minutes the mound was destroyed, caving in toward the central den.

I saw Kamala's feet sticking out of the heaped dirt, and I leaped into the center, throwing clods every which way. In moments I had uncovered her head and began brushing the dirt from her mouth and eyes.

Mr. Welles stepped over the fallen walls to help.

"No," I said, pushing him away. I picked up Kamala's body and cradled it in my arms. She was not heavy at all, and I could feel her breathing against me. "I will carry her home myself."

We were a strange processional. Ahead of me went Mr. Welles and Rama, to hold bushes and thorns out of the way. Behind came the carters and the villagers, guns ready, for we were fairly deep into the sal and one can never tell when a tiger with her cubs might be on the path.

We walked nearly two hours, and not once did I put Kamala down or let anyone else touch her. And then we crossed the puddles where the mahseer swam along

the pebbly bottom, and I knew we were close to The
Home. All at once Kamala felt heavy, but still I would
not let her go.

Ahead I could see the walled house. The gate was
open, and there were many figures in front of it, jostling
for position.

Mrs. Welles stood in front, and with her were all the
children except Indira, who had been banished inside.
Even Cook was there, patting little straggles of hair back
into her braid.

When we got close, Mrs. Welles reached out as if to
take Kamala from me, but I shook my head and walked
past her into the courtyard. I marched with Kamala's
body in my arms to her little hut and set her down
carefully onto the floor.

"Kamala," I said, patting the ground beside her.
"Home. We are home."

Her eyes opened. She looked up at me, a long steady
gaze, directly into my eyes.

"Mmmmmdas," she said, then closed her eyes again.
It was the last word she ever spoke.

# ENDINGS
# AND BEGINNINGS

♦♦♦

LIFE WENT ON AT THE HOME BUT KAMALA WAS NO LONGER any real part of it. She played and ate with the dogs again and adopted a particularly nasty bantam rooster as her special friend. She pounced on lizards and mice, ate dirt and pebbles after each meal, rolled in dead wood pigeons, and buried their bones near her hut. Yet she seemed, somehow, content. At night there were no more howls or moans except on the full of the moon, though she often took to prowling the compound until dawn, as restless as a jungle beast in a zoo.

Word of her got out, first through the village men, then by Dr. Singh's recitation at a dinner party. The newspapers printed stories, mostly inaccurate, about her discovery and her life at The Home. Mr. Welles' report to the Diocese did little to dam the rising tide of gossip. An enterprising photographer, turned down in his request for pictures, scaled the compound wall one night. Kamala bit him on the leg, and he lost his camera while making his escape. But still the papers continued to seek her out, and as a consequence of stories in the *Calcutta Statesman* and the popular London daily the *Westminster Gazette,* she received several proposals of marriage, a number of suggestions for cures (including one from a gentleman from Bombay who advocated hanging her upside down to "improve her brain faculties"), and a long letter offering her a chance to star in a film. From the Psychological Society in New York came an invitation for a tour. Mr. Welles saved the letters, but did not trouble to answer them, except one from King George V, which he had framed and hung in his study.

What happened the rest of the year I do not know firsthand, for I was sent off to school in England, to Sandhurst, Mr. Welles' old alma mater, on a scholarship arranged by him. I was more homesick there for the smell of jasmine and sewlee than I ever could have imagined, and I was treated like some sort of strange dark animal by the boys and the masters.

When I came home briefly for a holiday, paid for by the Diocesan Council because my grades had been the highest in my form, Kamala was dead of a parasite picked up from one of the pigeons she had eaten. She had been buried next to Amala under a large banyan tree in the church cemetery. I put flowers on her grave, flowers that I picked deep in the sal. I wrapped their stems with a bright red string. Only I really mourned her; the others scarcely seemed to notice she was gone.

Then I returned to England, where I stayed until my schooling was complete.

I became a writer, a lover of words, and took a first in the study of languages at Oxford. But until this book I never once wrote about Kamala, for over the years I learned that what is true and what is real are sometimes difficult to distinguish and that memory blurs the line even more. Still, I lived with the wolf-girl in a time and in a place that is the stuff of memory and of dream, and because I had the words to tell of it I—at least—have never forgotten.

# WHAT IS TRUE
# ABOUT THIS BOOK

◆◆◆

ON OCTOBER 9, 1920, THE REVEREND J. A. L. SINGH, AN INDIAN
missionary and rector of The Orphanage in Midnapore
India, led a party of hunters into the sal jungle. Their
express purpose was to discover what was haunting the
Santal village of Godamuri, for the Reverend Mr. Singh,
known as a mighty hunter, had been asked by one of
the village leaders, a man named Chunarem, to help.

The Singh party found two children in a wolf's den
that was carved out of a white ant mound. Along with
the children, they discovered a mother wolf and her
cubs. They shot the large wolf, sold off the cubs, and
the Reverend Mr. Singh brought the two children back

with him after they had been almost starved to death by the superstitious and frightened villagers.

Amala and Kamala, as they were named, lived very much like animals at first, eating raw meat, swallowing gravel, gnawing bones. They ran on all fours and refused to wear clothing. The most startling part of the story was that their eyes apparently glowed with blue lights in the dark.

A year later, on September 21, 1921, Amala died. Kamala lived on at the Singh orphanage another eight years, dying on November 14, 1929. I have, for the sake of the novel, telescoped Kamala's progress. In reality she did not start to walk upright for two and a half years or to speak for three. She did not have the semblance of a regular vocabulary until 1924, and even as late as 1926 that vocabulary consisted of only thirty words.

For purposes of contrast and characterization, I have turned the Reverend Mr. Singh into a British minister and given him a British wife, and made up a whole cast of fictional orphans as well. Mohandas Jinnah did not exist in The Orphanage, nor did Rama, Preeti, Indira, Veda, or Krithi. But the wolf-girls did, and my descriptions of them and what they did come from the Reverend Mr. Singh's own diary, published in a book entitled *Wolf-Children and Feral Man* (Harper and Brothers, 1939, 1941, 1942). Further information about them I gleaned from Charles Maclean's brilliant book *The*

*Wolf-Children* (Hill and Wang, 1978), and newspaper accounts of the time. My information about India's folk-life and its jungle life came from innumerable books on folklore and wildlife, though I want to cite especially Robert McClung's *Rajpur, Last of the Bengal Tigers* (Morrow, 1982). I also had the invaluable help of Dr. Krithivasan Ramamritham, who read my book in manuscript.

The Reverend Mr. Singh's remarkable diary, with its accompanying photographs of the wolf-children, caused a great deal of controversy in the scientific communities from the day it was published. It was championed by such experts as child psychologist Arnold Gesell and called a complete hoax by others. But for the purposes of this novel, I have assumed that the diary is totally and unassailably accurate. Whether Singh exaggerated or not, I do not care, for, as Emily Dickinson once wrote, "I dwell in possibility."                    —J.Y.

Jane Yolen is the award-winning author of more than seventy books, including *Simple Gifts* and *The Gift of Sarah Barker* (both Viking). She grew up in a family of storytellers. "It's no wonder that I love to tell tales," she says. "Other people might call it lying, but our family valued a fabulist."

Dr. Yolen has written articles and essays on feral children and the development of language. Several years ago, at a book auction, she bought a rare copy of an original missionary's diary, and she became fascinated with the wolf-girls of India. She says that *Children of the Wolf* is "both historical and a fantasy. There are many scientists who question whether the girls really lived as cubs. But what concerns me is the boy, Mohandas—whom I invented—and how he responds to the wolf children, learning that language and love can set him free."

A graduate of Smith College, Jane Yolen now teaches children's literature there. She lives with her husband and their three teenagers on a farm in Hatfield, Massachusetts.